# Chasing Sunsets

The Bonds that Endure Beyond the Setting Sun

By

## John Derek Ruffin

BOOK WRITING
PIONEER

# Acknowledgement

I'd like to thank my sisters, Rhonda and Susan, for their input in the story, as well as my niece, April. I'd also like to thank my 8th - grade teacher, Joan Thomas, who was the first to read a rough draft of the story and offer suggestions. Finally, My Dad, Johnny and my Aunt Dot, who were the inspiration behind John and Clover.

# Dedication

For my sweet Mother Joan Brooks Ruffin. A Godly woman who loved her family with a fierce dedication and was happiest when we were together.

KAROLINE SCHNEIDER
KARL SCHNEIDER
JULIA YOUNG
JACK YOUNG
CORA CAMPBELL
THOMAS CAMPBELL
MARY YOUNG FOSTER MOTHER
CLYDE YOUNG FOSTER FATHER
KATHERINE CAMPBELL
ASA CAMPBELL
S CAMPBELL
CORA CAMPBELL
MADIOLA CAMPBELL
JOHN CAMPBELL
VIOLA PIERSON
RAYMOND PIERSON
JULIE CAMPBELL
ROBERT CAMPBELL
DOROTHY SIMPSON
ALEX SIMPSON
AMY DELA CRUZ
BROOKS CAMPBELL
JENNA LANGDON
ANDREW LANGDON
JACOB CAMPBELL
BLAKE CAMPBELL
JOSEPH CAMPBELL
Campbell Family Tree

# Table of Contents

# Chapter 1

---

**C****huck** Langdon has known the Campbell Family of Sullivan County, Georgia, for as long as he can remember. His father used to say, "The Campbells don't just run this county – they run through it like a river that keeps everything alive." For Chuck, the Campbells are more than neighbors; they are a part of his identity. While his experience is limited to 49 years, the families have shared close bonds for over a hundred years when his great-grandfather, Joseph Langdon, came to Sullivan County in 1918 with his young wife, Myrtice, and settled as tenant farmers on the Campbell farm. Chuck often wonders what Joseph would think if he saw their families now, still intertwined, still shaping each other. The Campbells have a rich and colorful history; many in the South Georgia community treasure them as friends and neighbors. They are an extraordinary family on many levels, and many consider themselves blessed to be called friends of the Campbells. They have a way of making people feel both included and indebted. "They are not just history," Chuck sometimes says, "they are a living monument to everyone they have touched."

Chuck is John Brooks Campbell's best friend. Like his father before, Chuck serves as legal counsel for Campbell Farms, Campbell Veterinary Hospital, and The Schneider Brewery. Brooks is the youngest of three children born to John Robert and Madiola Brooks Campbell. Their other two children are James Robert (Bobby) and Dorothy (Dottie) Campbell Simpson. Bobby and Dottie are two years apart, with Brooks being five years younger than Dottie. Their ages are 56, 54 and 49, respectively. Each of the Campbell Children lives in Sullivan County with their families. ***Bobby and Brooks*** - work for the Schneider Brewery and Campbell Farms, which comprises 3,500 acres of cropland, pastureland, pecan groves, and a successful brewery. ***Dottie***, a veterinarian - works with her aunt Velma (Clover) Campbell Pierson, also a veterinarian. Together, they operate a large and small animal practice at the farm.

John Campbell, the family patriarch, sees life in two distinct phases – before Madie and after Madie. He retired from the brewery and much of the farming soon after his sweet Madie passed away suddenly, a month shy of their 50th wedding anniversary in 2015. For a man who had spent decades solving problems and managing crises, her sudden departure was one thing he couldn't fix. John was 70 and Madie 69 at the time of her death. Madie Campbell had always been the picture of health, so her diagnosis of atrial fibrillation felt more like a suggestion than a sentence. Although medicated and under a doctor's supervision, she collapsed one August morning, watering her beloved hibiscus and birds of paradise around their pool. Had he been there, John would have half-expected her to rise, brush herself off, and laugh it off as if it were nothing. But she didn't. An autopsy later showed Madie died of a massive embolic stroke. John would often sit by that very pool, looking at the flowers she had tended to, wondering how he was supposed to tend to life without her.

Sally Hubert, a neighbor and close friend, stopped by to collect Madie for their morning stroll and discovered her lifeless body lying on the pool deck. Henry and Sally Hubert, a black couple, have lived on the Campbell Farm since they married over 50 years ago. Born and raised on the farm, Henry worked for the Campbells before retiring.

John Campbell and his children are descendants of Asa Louis Campbell, a Scottish immigrant. In May of 1910, Asa Campbell stepped off the S.S. Fernandina and onto the shores of Savannah, Georgia, carrying more than just cargo. The Fernandina was a freighter-class ship that serviced a route from England to Charleston and Savannah. Although not a passenger vessel, the Fernandina had a few passenger cabins available for those wishing to travel with their cargo. Asa booked a ticket for travel as a representative of the Grange Distillery in Burntisland, Scotland. The Grange was one of Scotland's largest distilleries at the time, with their primary market being the United States. Although Asa was supposedly traveling on business, he had no intention of making a return trip. When Asa stepped off the ship onto River Street in Savannah, he could barely contain his excitement.

With his cargo being readied for rail shipment, Asa walked along the various city squares, his footsteps slow, as if pulled by the allure of Savannah's natural beauty. Towering oaks stretched their ancient arms overhead, their branches adorned with cascading curtains of Spanish moss that swayed gently in the warm breeze. Beneath them, azaleas exploded in vibrant hues, their petals a riot of pinks, reds and purples, painting the streets. Asa, mesmerized, paused to take in the scene – the way the sun filtered through the leaves, dappling the ground in soft, golden light. The air was alive with the sweet scent of blossoms and the melodic trills of unseen songbirds.  He stood captivated as a hummingbird, a flicker of emerald and sapphire, darted between the blooms, its delicate wings humming in a blur of motion, feeding from the rich floral tapestry that lined the streets. The world here felt larger, more vibrant than anything he had ever known, and in that moment, Asa felt as though he had stepped into a place teeming with life and endless possibilities.

Another first for Asa was seeing so many negroes in one place. Being Scottish, Asa had minimal experience with black people. Asa knew, as much as any Scotsman, about the American Civil War and slavery. Still, he assumed most blacks went north after the war. However, from what he was seeing, they most certainly did not. Soon enough, the young immigrant reached the Savannah Depot and met his cargo of 25 barrels and 150 cases, each containing six half-gallon bottles of Old Burntisland Scotch Whisky. Soon, he was traveling west on the Central of Georgia Railroad headed for Sullivan County, Georgia.

Campbell, an only child raised by his father, Thomas Campbell, was orphaned at four years old when Thomas succumbed to injuries incurred from a fall while working for the Grange Distillery in Burntisland, a small village in the county of Fife in Scotland. Thomas, a single parent, lost his wife Cora two days following Asa's birth. Thomas and Cora were only children, leaving no family to care for Asa. The chief distiller, Clyde Young, was quite fond of Thomas, so he and his wife, Mary Ruthven Young, took Asa in, not wanting to see the lad end up in an orphanage. The Youngs were a childless couple in their mid-forties when Asa came to live with them. Their home, though modest, carried the warmth of years spent together – its wooden beams creaked with age, and the smell of fresh bread often lingered in the air, mixing with the earthly scent of hay and livestock. The animals provided a simple rhythm of the Youngs' lives – the lowing of cattle at dawn, the cluck of chicken scratching in the dirt.

Asa loved the animals and was tending to the chores of feeding, watering, and milking by his sixth birthday. When he wasn't busy with school or farm chores, he was at Clyde's side at the distillery. As Asa grew into a young man, much was learned from his foster father about the distillation process. He had yet to know how valuable those skills would prove a few years later.

The farm, however, was Asa's first love. Asa felt an almost spiritual connection to the animals and land. He loved planting the seeds and watching the crops flourish. By his 12th birthday, Asa had built new fences, expanded cropland, and showed a modest income from his labor. Although the Youngs never officially adopted young Asa, they loved and treated him as their own. As a toddler learning to speak, Asa developed a habit of repeating his words; he referred to them as Kide Kide and Mare Mare. Mary was a gifted musician and taught Asa how to play the violin. By his teens, he was a great fiddle player.

In the summer of 1908, Clyde Young's brother, Jack, with his wife Julia and daughter Katherine (Katie), visited their kin and stayed with the family for over a month while touring his Scottish homeland. Jack Young had immigrated to America in his early 20s and ended up settling in southern Georgia along the Thronateeska River. The lush, sprawling landscape reminded him of the Scottish hills in its own way, though the southern heat was a stark contrast. Jack Young ran a successful farm and brewery in Georgia, started by his father-in-law, Karl Schneider, in 1892.

Young met the Schneider family by chance on his westbound journey in 1890. A German immigrant, Karl had secured an opportunity to buy land along the Thronateeska River in southern Georgia. With no sons of his own, he found Jack likable and very mature for his age. Before long, he introduced him to his wife Karoline and daughter Julia. By the journey's end, Jack was like an old friend and had taken a keen liking to Julia, five years his junior. Upon arriving in Baltimore in September 1890, Schneider, knowing he would need able-bodied help to get his idea off the ground, invited Jack to travel with the family to Georgia.

Within two years, Jack and Julia had gotten married, and Karl had his farm and brewery in operation along the Thronateeska. Their product, called Schneider Bock, a lager, is still brewed along the river today. In 1905, at Young's suggestion, Schneider began importing Scotch. During the early 1900s in America, whisky was sold in barrels and bottles directly from distilleries to bars, hotels, restaurants, and private individuals, mainly through mail order. Alongside his brewery, Schneider had created a niche market, blending various spirits and enhancing them with sugar, spices, and other herbal blends to broaden their appeal. He distributed his products throughout Georgia, Alabama, and Florida. The beer and spirits business had grown exceptionally profitable for Schneider and Young; by 1910, they were the South's primary importer of scotch whisky. This arrangement with the Grange Distillery brought Asa to Sullivan County.

The Young family reunion was indeed a joyous one. The two brothers hadn't seen each other in almost 20 years. Clyde and Mary were married when Jack departed Scotland, but they had only met Julia, Katie, and Asa by exchanging letters. When the families weren't traveling around the countryside or visiting Edinburgh, Clyde and Jack spent time together at the distillery. Mary and Julia bonded over the warm hearth of the kitchen, spending long afternoons sharing cherished family recipes and exchanging tips on cooking practices passed down through generations. Mary, with her Scottish heritage, introduced Julia to hearty stews and delicate pastries, while Julia brought the flavors of her German upbringing – savory sausages, freshly baked bread, and tangy pickled vegetables. Meanwhile, Clyde and Mary loved hearing tales about life in America.

While initially shy around each other, the new "cousins," Asa and Katie, soon spent their free time exploring Asa's haunts around Fife. Asa was quite sure he had never seen such a beautiful girl. 15-year-old Katie was a gorgeous young woman with curly strawberry-blonde hair, peach skin, girlish freckles, and grey-blue eyes. At 16, Asa was approaching 6 ft tall and towered almost a foot over Katie. He had a lean yet muscular build, wavy-sandy blond hair, blue eyes, and pocks of freckles on each ruddy cheek, giving him an innocent boyish look.

Asa showed Katie all his choice spots around Burntisland. Their favorite site was the beach and waterfront overlooking the North Sea, especially at sunset. It wasn't long before they found themselves holding hands and walking barefoot in the cold surf, sharing stories and dreams they each had. As time progressed, each began to dread the sting that would most certainly occur at the month's end when

Katie had to leave for America. The day before her departure, they spent one more evening together at the beach in each other's arms, shedding silent tears and fighting back the pain of heartbreak. The youngster's affection for each other didn't go unnoticed by the adults. While not encouraged, it wasn't necessarily discouraged either. Behind the scenes, Mary and Julia noticed how handsome the young couple was, reminding them of their courtship days.

On May 18, 1910, 18-year-old Asa arrived at the Ashland, Georgia Depot, and waiting on the platform was beautiful Katie. Asa jumped from the moving train onto the platform and into Katie's arms, the world around them fading into the background. The two prior years had been the longest and hardest of their young lives, and they didn't even try to hold back their tears of joy. Asa buried his face in her hair, breathing in the familiar scent he had missed so deeply, while Katie clung to him as if afraid that if she let go, he might disappear again. No words were needed- everything they felt poured out in that single embrace.

After securing the cargo, Asa and the Youngs were en route to the farm and brewery. Once they arrived and unloaded the whisky, Jack and Katie gave Asa a property tour. Asa was impressed by the neatness of the operation and loved the new scenery, especially the redhead walking beside him. The brewery was built along the high river bluffs of the Thronateeska in North Sullivan County. The Schneider Brewery was constructed from locally sourced cypress and long-leaf pine lumber. The exterior had cypress clapboard siding and a metal roof. At the roof's ridge were raised letters spelling "Schneider." A covered front porch ran the entire length of the building, with a grain bin at one end and a large cast iron pipe at the end near the river. At the base of the river bluffs was a large blue hole, the sole supply of fresh water for the brewery.

Just as in Savannah, he was experiencing new sights and sounds, including hearing his first bobwhite quail, whippoorwills, and the peaceful hum of cicadas later that evening. He found Sullivan County and the Thronateeska River more beautiful than he had imagined.

The next couple of days were spent getting Asa acquainted with the farm and brewery and settling into his new home. Although the Youngs had room in their home for Asa, there was no way, under the canopies of heaven, Julia would have the two youngsters under the same roof. Therefore, Asa moved his meager belongings into a vacant tenant house on the farm.

On Saturday afternoon, Asa and Katie rode horseback to another blue hole along the west bank of the Thronateeska. Blue holes are deep underground springs along rivers. If the spring is strong enough, it displaces the surface water sufficiently to create an oasis of cold, clear water in a mostly stained river flow and, for centuries, has served as a source of clean water and recreation. The water temperature is approximately 70 degrees year-round. Asa was amazed by the spot's natural beauty upon reaching the river. Large live oak and cypress trees draped in Spanish moss towered stately along the riverbank. For the first time, Asa spotted a nearby alligator. He valiantly ushered Katie behind him, placing his body between her and the reptile. Seeing his anxiousness, Katie said, "Asa darling, the gators are of no concern, I assure you." While he wanted to defer to her expertise, he was relieved when the prehistoric-looking critter entered the river and slowly swam away.

Katie had prepared pork sandwiches, potato salad, and sweet tea for the picnic. This particular blue hole was her favorite. The shallow riverbank was covered in limestone, creating a rock beach that gradually descended into the cold waters of the blue hole. After eating, Katie and Asa dipped into the cool river, splashing each other and laughing like they hadn't in years. The sunlight dappled through the trees and as they waded back to shore, droplets of water sparkled on their skin. Back on the blanket, they lay side by side, hands just inches apart, as if each was waiting for the other to bridge the gap. Katie was the first to move, her fingers tentatively brushing against Asa's. He caught her hand in his, gently, as if testing whether this connection still felt as natural as it once had. His thumb traced small circles along her knuckles, a touch both familiar and thrilling. It was as if they were discovering each other all over again, with a mixture of excitement and reverence.

Asa shifted onto his side, gazing at her with a softness she hadn't seen in years. He reached up, tucking a strand of damp hair behind her ear, his hand lingering near her face. And then, with a gentle breath, he leaned down and kissed her. It was hesitant at first, just a whisper of a kiss as if he were waiting for her to pull away. But Katie's hand moved to his shoulder, pulling him closer, and his kiss deepened, speaking the words they hadn't said aloud.

When they finally pulled back, he looked at her with a hint of awe, as though even he couldn't quite believe they'd found their way back to this moment. His fingers trailed slowly down her arm, lingering as they brushed over her wrist, her skin tingling beneath his touch. Katie felt a blush spread over her cheeks, her heart racing with a mix of anticipation and familiarity. His hand remained on hers, fingers grazing her knuckles as if he were rediscovering every inch of her, unearthing feelings they'd both thought were long buried.

The world around them grew quiet, the soft hum of the afternoon air a gentle backdrop to their shared breath, their closeness. She couldn't resist sliding her hand up his arm, her fingers tracing over the subtle strength of his muscles, the warmth beneath his skin. Each touch was a question, and with every return glance, every shy smile, they both answered without words.

Katie drew closer, and Asa moved his hand to her face, his palm warm against her cheek as he brushed his thumb just beneath her eyes, his gaze never leaving hers. He tilted his head, studying her as if he wanted to memorize every detail, every line and curve that made her uniquely his. When he leaned in again, his kiss was slower this time, deeper—a gentle but deliberate promise. She let her hands slide up, wrapping around his neck, pulling him closer, and for a long, breathless moment, there was nothing in the world but the taste of his kiss, the warmth of his hands, the soft press of his body against hers.

They lay back together on the blanket, their legs tangled, faces close enough that she could see every fleck of color in his eyes. He ran his fingers slowly up her arm, leaving a trail of goosebumps in their wake, and she shivered, her breath hitching in her throat.

The past melted away, leaving only the present, this shared space where nothing else mattered.

As the sun dropped behind the curtain of cypress and oak trees, their fingers explored each other with a kind of tenderness, rediscovering paths long forgotten, mapping each curve, each touch, as if every sensation were new. She let her hand rest on his chest, feeling the steady thrum of his heartbeat beneath her palm, a reminder of the quiet strength she'd always admired. He pulled her closer, his breath warm against her neck, his lips grazing her skin in a way that sent shivers down her spine. Katie looked up into his eyes, and in that shared gaze, she saw not just the boy she once loved but the man who would be her protector, provider, lover, and the father of her future children. The realization settled over her, solid and warm, filling her with a quiet certainty. She knew in that instant that she was safe, cherished, and wanted, and as she reached for him, she felt herself surrendering completely, relinquishing any hesitation.

Their breaths mingled, becoming one, as they let go of everything but this moment, their bodies and hearts moving in sync. There was no rush, only the deep, unhurried rhythm of two souls finding their way back to one another. Beneath the open sky, with only the swaying tree branches as witnesses, they shared a love that was both familiar and electric, grounding and exhilarating.

When they finally lay together in silence, his hand rested gently on her waist, her head tucked beneath his chin, both enveloped in a profound peace. She could feel his thumb tracing soft circles on her hip, the lingering warmth of his touch reassuring her in a way that words never could. He pressed one last, lingering kiss to her forehead, and in the quiet, she closed her eyes, knowing that this— right here in his arms—was where she was meant to be, today and for all the days that would follow.

Afterward, the two fell asleep, only to wake upon hearing one of the horses' neighs. Time had slipped up on the two, and the sun was beginning to set. After dressing and mounting the horses, they rode along the trail back towards the Young's home. Along the way, they stopped to enjoy the sunset. Asa stepped off his mare, looked at Katie, and said, "Katie, we've seen some pretty sunsets together in two countries. While this may not be the most splendid, we've enjoyed together, this one is ours for now and always if you will be my wife". Katie was already his in her heart, but she replied, "Asa, you are mine now and forever, darling, so yes, a thousand times yes!"

# Chapter 2

**F**ollowing Madie's untimely death and funeral in 2015, John Campbell was alone for the first time and took his bride's death hard. He felt an emptiness he had never known before. The love of his life, the woman with whom he had built dreams, was gone, leaving behind only silence in the home they once filled with laughter and plans for the future. Her absence felt like a weight pressing down on his chest, making it hard to breathe and hard to think. Every corner of their house reminded him of her – the kitchen where they would talk for hours, the bedroom that now felt colder, larger, without her warmth beside him.

The day Madie passed, Clover, a widow herself, stayed the night with John in the home where they were both raised, and the two are still roommates to this day. She had lost her husband years before, and perhaps that was why she knew that John needed most wasn't words but presence. The kind of presence that silently understood the grief without pushing him to speak when the words would only crumble on his lips. Her quiet presence was an anchor in his storm of sorrow.

While all the Campbells are very close, the twins are so exceptionally. Velma was given the nickname "Clover" by her father, Asa. As a toddler watching her play with the rough and tumble boys, he remarked to his Katie how tough she was. He said, "That girl's like white Dutch clover, pretty but tough." Asa and Katie Campbell had four children but lost the oldest two before John and Clover were born. Their most senior, Cora, died from leukemia in the early 30s, and their son, Thomas, was killed in action during WWII, leaving them childless at 48 and 52 years old. However, at 49 years old, Katie found herself pregnant. While the two were concerned at their advanced age, they were thrilled at the opportunity to become parents once again. They were overjoyed when the twins arrived healthy on December 16, 1945.

Still a licensed vet at 77, Clover works part-time at the vet practice. Her days are filled with the familiar scent of hay and animals, the hum of the clinic offering her a sense of purpose even in her last years. But her story began long before the vet practice, when she lost her husband, Ray, in 1968 when the F4 Phantom he was piloting went down in Vietnam. The news of his death was like a sharp crack in her world, leaving her with a hole that seemed impossible to fill. At the time of Ray's death, Clover worked as a nurse for the Balboa Naval Hospital in San Diego. After losing Ray, Clover couldn't find a reason to stay in California and was soon headed east to Sullivan County in the 1968 Lincoln Continental Ray had purchased before being deployed to Vietnam. The car was both a painful reminder of her loss and a symbol of their love – a gift she could never bring herself to part with. The road stretched out before her, each mile pulling her further from the life they had planned together. By the time she reached Sullivan County, she was a woman in search of not just a place to call home but a way to piece herself back together.

Within a year, she applied and was accepted into veterinary school in Athens, Georgia. Clover had always loved the family pets and livestock, so the family wasn't surprised at her decision and encouraged it, hoping it would give her something to focus on besides Ray's passing. Furthermore, having a vet in the family wouldn't hurt. Upon graduation from vet school, Clover returned home and opened Campbell Animal Hospital on the farm. Today, it's one of the busiest veterinary practices in the area.

Although retired from the day-to-day operation of the farm and brewery, John serves as an advisor to his two sons and a brand ambassador for the brewery. Schneider Bock is a copper-colored, full-bodied, smooth-drinking lager and remains the brewery's main product. Schneider is in the top ten of privately owned breweries in the US, with Schneider Bock being commonplace as Bud and Miller in the southern states with more recent placement in a few markets out west. While Schneider Beer isn't the number one beer consumed locally, it's a close third. The retail cost of Schneider is approximately 20% more than popular brands by Anheuser Busch, Miller and Coors due to the immense volumes produced by the big breweries, which keep their cost down. Until 20 years ago, the brewery made one product, Schneider Bock. However, John Campbell was encouraged by his sons and management team to add more offerings to enhance sales. A light beer called Schlight was introduced first and soon became a huge hit, almost surpassing sales of the original brew. Later on, seasonal brews were added, such as Schneider Georgia Peach Summertime and Schneider Fall Brew, a red-hued, sweeter take on classic Schneider.

While the Campbell family has done exceptionally well, they live relatively modest lives. Each lives in simple but well-kept homes large enough to meet family needs. The largest residence on the property is the original homeplace of Asa and Katie Campbell, where John and Clover currently reside. It's a 3,800-square-foot Greek Revival, towering at the heart of the Campbell estate, is a monument to generations of memories, its very bones echoing with the laughter and stories of those who have come before. The house stands with a quiet dignity, its stately presence anchored by six grand columns that frame the wide, sweeping front porch. Weathered but solid, the columns have stood the test of time, much like the family itself, enduring both joy and sorrow under its sheltering roof.

The Campbell children live in homes they've built or remodeled family homes from the previous generations. Bobby, his wife Julie and son Joe live in John and Madie's former house, where Bobby was raised. Dottie lives with her husband, Alex Simpson, and daughter, Jenna, in Karl and Karoline's two-story Queen Anne. Brooks lives in a two-bedroom barndominium he built himself after finishing college.

Brooks is the only child of John and Madie, unmarried. However, he is the father of a 17-year-old son, Jake. Jake's mother, Amy, is a beautiful Filipino from Colleton County next door. Brooks and Amy dated years ago but never married. Amy's father, a local surgeon, was strictly opposed to the relationship from the start, insisting she marry only men of her race.

Furthermore, Brooks wasn't a Catholic, which was another deal-breaker. Although Brooks wanted to seal the relationship and loved Amy, she relented to her father's wishes. They remain close friends, committed to raising Jake as Mom and Dad. Amy still lives locally and remains single as well. As a matter of fact, neither have had a serious relationship since Jake came along.

A popular spot on the Campbell's estate is the "Pump House." Originally built as a service station for fueling farm equipment and vehicles, it also served as a local store for the farm and locals as recently as the early 90s. The fuel tanks are empty now, but the two 1940s Tokheim pumps remain, restored to like new condition with Texaco "Fire Chief" labeling and lighted displays. The site currently serves as a gathering place for family and friends. The interior is outfitted with a few pieces of Schneider memorabilia, such as framed adverts from the brewery's early days and some old family portraits. Several antique chairs surround a weathered table where a chandelier hangs above, fashioned from empty Schneider bottles. A time and heat-hardened pot-belied stove and a rusty 1950s Kelvinator fridge keep the house warm in winter and beer cold year-round. Another memorabilia item is a family favorite, a signed and framed Bellamy Brothers poster from 1992 promoting a company concert during the 100th farm and brewery anniversary. John Campbell loves The Bellamys and was thrilled when they agreed to play at the event. At the rear of the Pump House, a large, covered porch overlooks one of the farm's pecan groves. At the end of almost any workday, you'll find the two Campbell Brothers, along with their father, sister, and Aunt Clover, at the Pump House.

Another regular is Henry "Rooster" Hubert. Henry and his wife Sally, or "Sweet" as she's referred to, live next to the Pump House in the same home Rooster was born in. Similar to the Campbell homes on the farm, it has seen its share of updates over the years—new plumbing, modern appliances, and fresh coats of paint—but in many ways, it remains the same. The creaky front porch still holds the weight of family gatherings, the kitchen still carries the smell of Sweet's famous blackberry cobbler, and the well-worn rocking chair where Rooster's father sat every evening to watch the sunset remains in its place, a silent witness to the passage of time.

Rooster is the third generation of a black sharecropper, also named Henry Hubert. Rooster and Sweet have one son, Grady, a successful cardio-thoracic surgeon at Emory University in Atlanta. Grady is two months younger than Bobby, and growing up together, they remain the closest of friends.

Rooster is quite the raconteur and has a mind sharp as a tack. His father called him "Rooster" because, as a young boy, he would often get up before his parents and walk through the house singing. John named him "Uncle Remus" after Bobby, Grady, and Dottie were born. Rooster would often sit with the children and spin his craft of storytelling while the children sat wide-eyed.

Not long ago, Chuck stopped by the Pump House after work and observed a typical gathering. Aunt Clover and John were on the back porch in rockers, surrounded by each other's dog companions. A red and white border collie named Jack and a brindle Scottish terrier named Daisy. Bobby, Brooks, and Rooster were inside giving little attention to the TV tuned to the Weather Channel. As Chuck walked in, Rooster said, "Well, if it isn't the local solicitor stopping by for a drink, what can we do for you, sir? Chuck tipped his hat and said I'd take whatever's cold, my friend, and found a seat next to Bobby. "What is that damn smell?" Chuck asked.

Brooks said, "Joe's in the bathroom." Joseph Campbell, Bobby's son, aged 25, soon appeared from the corner bathroom as if he'd slayed a dragon. As he closed the door, he scraped his boots on the floor, as a dog does when making a satisfactory deposit.

Brooks laughed, looked at his brother, and said, "Bobby, I hate to be the one to tell you this, but something has crawled, but more likely been placed up your boy's ass and died!"

Looking at Joe, he says, "Have you ever heard of a damn courtesy flush?"

Joe smiled at his uncle and said, "Brookie, you're just jealous 'cause you done got old and can't take a good ole shit anymore." All laughed, and the group moved outside on the back porch, where each man, almost in unison, placed a dip of snuff in their cheek. Bobby instructed Joe to ride to the farm store and grab some ground beef for the group to make burgers later.

By sunset, every Campbell was accounted for: John and Clover, along with John's three children, two in-laws, three grandchildren, Henry and Sweet, and several dogs. After supper, Brooks sat in the pump house with his eight-year-old Scottie, Hank, by his side. Just to his right was his sister-in-law, Julie. Brooks and Julie are very close, each looking at the other as siblings. After all, he was only eleven when she came into the family and treated him nicer than his brother and sister.

Julie asked, "Brookie, when are you and Amy gonna shit or get off the pot?"

He smiled in recognition of the question and replied, "Darlin, if I knew, I swear before all that is Holy, I would tell you. All I can say is we both seem content with how things are, and I'm not questioning it."

Julie smiled, stood up, and gave him an overhead bear hug from behind, kissing him on the cheek. Brooks, lightly grasping her forearms, looked up and said, "I'm happy, I know that. There should be a law against being as happy as I am?" She laughed and said, "Baby, there are some laws against some of the shit you smoke that makes you happy!"

Outside, the remaining Campbells had gathered around a fire pit. Rooster is the official fire tender and keeps dry firewood nearby for such an occasion. Joe and two cousins stood while the older generation took up the available chairs. The other cousins were Dottie's daughter, Jenna, and Brook's son Jake.

One thing that makes the Campbell family exceptional is their commitment to family. Each Campbell grandchild is immersed in other family members' lives from a young age, creating an environment of familiarity, appreciation, and dependence. As anyone marrying into the family will tell you, if you're unwilling to share them with the family, move along because that part isn't negotiable.

Brooks appears from the pump house, packing a can of Copenhagen. After placing a generous dip in his left bottom cheek, he announced to everyone, "I'm so glad all our family are here because I intend to announce that my son, your grandson, and nephew informed me he intends to be a Georgia Game Warden. You heard it right, my boy endeavors to join the Paw Patrol!" Everyone laughed and turned to Jake as he glanced up at his father with a half-crooked smile and a look each knew to say, "You Asshole."

Jake said, "All I said to Dad was I think it would be a cool job to be a game warden." Uncle Alex looks at his nephew and says, "Boy, surely you know this family's history with the rabbit police.

You know damn well the law don't go 'round here. From the time of your great granddaddy, those bastards have been nothing short of a nuisance." Alex referred to a few tense altercations the Campbell men have shared with the Department of Natural Resource Officers over the years.

A popular story Bobby tells from his childhood involves such an encounter. As the story goes, Bobby was sitting on the front porch one sweltering summer morning in the mid-70s, with his Paw Paw, Asa, rocking slowly in his favorite chair. A young Georgia Game Warden pulled up his state-issued green Ford pickup, dust swirling in the air as the truck came to a stop. The warden stepped out, all business, and walked up to the porch with a serious look on his face and asked if he was Asa Campbell. In his still-evident Scottish accent, Campbell replied, "Well, that's what they tell me, young man; what can I do for you?"

The warden cleared his throat, "Well, Mr. Campbell, it's been reported you have been shooting at deer on your property out of season."

Asa replied, "Well, I don't know what season you refer to. Only two around here are salt and pepper, but damn right, I've put a load of shot in several of em's asses. Sons of bitches are eating my peas." He spat the last word out like it was a personal offense.

The officer said, "Well, Mr. Campbell, you need to get a permit for shooting deer out of season."

Asa replied, "Is that a fact? Well, give me a permit." He crossed his arms, challenging the young warden to stand his ground.

"Well, you'll have to get it from the courthouse." the warden explained.

Asa shook his head and said, "Boy, I go to the courthouse once a year to pay my taxes and don't plan on going again till this November, but I tell you what, since you're so interested, I figure them deer must belong to you, so I'll permit you to go on my property anytime you want. Keep up with how many peas they eat and pay me $3 per bushel, and I'll put my shotgun away."

The game warden replied, "Mr. Campbell, I don't need your permission to go on your property."

The 85-year-old Campbell stood up from his rocker, chest poked out with both hands firmly on his hips, and said, "Well, now damned if it don't look like you're trying to get a load of shot in your ass!" His voice was calm, but the threat hung in the air like the humidity before a summer storm.

Knowing his grandfather's short fuse with bureaucrats, Bobby knew they would soon be headed to jail. He could already imagine the two of them carted off in the back of that green pickup, his Paw Paw railing against the government the entire way. However, the officer relented, got in his truck, and rode away, returning later in the day with Paw Paw's deer permit.

# Chapter 3

Today, the Campbell property utilized for income purposes incorporates the 25-acre brewery grounds, which has grown into a regional attraction known for its quality brews, 200 acres of fenced and cross-fenced beef cattle pastures, barns to store hay, feed, and equipment, and a 2500-square-foot meat processing facility.

The cattle operation passed down through generations has been a cornerstone of the family's success, blending tradition with modern sustainability practices. In addition, 1500 acres are held for barley production and another 100 acres for pecan tree orchards. The remaining acreage is dedicated solely to wildlife and conservation.

All the Campbell men are avid sportsmen and devote considerable time, energy, and money to enhancing wildlife habitat on their property. Brooks and Bobby have spent a small fortune on the re-establishment of bobwhite quail on the farm. Their efforts, often involving long hours in the field, have started to pay off as the quail population slowly rebounds. Several acres of the land border the upper end of 8,300-acre Lake Early, where the shallow water is dotted with hundreds of cypress trees and stumps following the damming of the Thronateeska in 1930. The eerie beauty of the cypress trees adds a unique charm to the landscape. The backwaters and sloughs of Lake Early produce some of the best duck hunting found in the state. The lake also provides excellent fishing and recreation for thousands of South Georgians.

The Campbells own a lakeside lodge on the upper end of Lake Early. Like many homes on the west side of the lake, the lodge is built on piers, with the first level below the flood plain. Although there hasn't been a catastrophic flood since 1994, building regulations require living spaces to be built above the flood level, which is eight feet above the ground on the Campbell property. The home's first level is half enclosed and half open. The enclosed portion is a climate-controlled storage room with fridges and freezers, two sets of bunk beds, and a full bathroom. The open half is screened in with a knee wall along the bottom. Several tables are set up for casual dining. The second and third floors incorporate a large, combined living and kitchen with four bedrooms and three and ½ baths. The lodge is decorated with deer head mounts taken over the years and one full body mount Bobby took in 2013. He had the taxidermist form the mount as if the large buck was jumping over the upstairs railing.

Several breeds of duck are displayed as well. The great room downstairs shows expertly prepared mounts of wood ducks, mallards, a blue-winged teal, and a red-breasted merganser. The lighting in the room has been carefully adjusted to highlight the intricate details of the birds, casting soft shadows that bring the mounts to life. On summer evenings, the smell of grilling steak fills the air as the family gathers around the outdoor kitchen, sipping ice-cold Schneider beer by the lakeside. Guests make their way to the dockside bar, where Bobby plays bartender, pouring drinks while kids splash in the lake. The outdoor kitchen is fully equipped, with stainless steel counters and a brick oven built into the stonework, seamlessly blending with the rustic charm of the lodge. The lodge is a family favorite and is used year-round, but it is bustling during the summertime when the family gathers to relax and enjoy each other's company. During summer months, the lodge's wide-open windows and large screened-in porch allow the cool lake breezes to flow through, offering relief from the Georgia heat.

Lake Early was built to provide low-cost hydroelectric power to the citizens of Sullivan and the surrounding counties and continues to supply hundreds of homes and businesses today. The Campbells lakeside property sits near the peaceful inflow of the Thronateeska River. Due to the stumps mentioned earlier, it's much quieter than the lower end of the lake. If one navigates a boat on the upper end of Lake Early, they better be sure of their surroundings. Otherwise, they are likely to replace a prop or worse.

The lake is active with boaters and sportsmen year-round, but a warm weather favorite is called the "sandbar." The sandbar is a section of the lake on the east shore with a sandy bottom. During summer weekends, 20-30 boats will be anchored with their occupants walking and swimming among the pontoons, ski boats, and jet skis in three-foot water. Music and the aromas from bar-b-que grills fill the air. Bobby, Dottie, Brooks, and their families are crowd regulars of the sandbar cartel. The family owns a Bentley Pontoon, a ten-year-old Bayliner wake boat, and a pair of Yamaha Waverunners. Drinking is the number one pastime at the sandbar, and Schneider beer is consumed by the gallons.

A popular bar and grill on the lake is called Booger Bottom. The official name is "Spring Creek Tavern," but no one refers to it as such. Most folks refer to it as "The Bottom." The bar is situated just south of the bridge, crossing Spring Creek Cove off Lake Early. That bridge crossing has always been referred to as Booger Bottom, so that's the name that stuck. It's open year-round, serving bottled and canned beer as well as the best hamburger in the state of Georgia. During the summer, the Bottom serves as a concert venue for local and national acts. The Swinging Medallions and The Atlanta Rhythm Section are crowd favorites.

The Campbell Family takes the stage at the Bottom a few weekends each year, drawing in a loyal crowd. Music runs deep in the family, much like their connection to the land, and it shows in the way they effortlessly blend instruments and harmonies. Whether it's Bobby switching between the smooth melodies of his acoustic guitar, the electrifying riffs of his electric, or the rich, soulful sound of his voice, he sets the tone for the night.

Dottie often commands the piano, her fingers dancing across the keys with the precision of someone who's been playing since childhood. When Brooks steps forward, guitar in hand, he brings a gritty edge, adding in the harmonica when the song calls for something a little more raw. Joe, even the rhythm master, holds it all together with his seamless transitions between guitar and drums, while Jake anchors the sounds with deep bass lines that shake the floorboards. Jenna, alternating between singing and piano with her mom, fills the room with her clear voice, harmonizing perfectly with Dottie and Brooks, their vocals weaving together effortlessly. Brooks has the widest vocal range of the guys and sings most numbers with Dottie and Jenna. They cover primarily 70s and 80s rock bands but throw some country in for flavor. Not too long ago, the family played at a wedding for a family friend's daughter. They covered the entire Rumours album by Fleetwood Mac.

# Chapter 4

**F**requent storytelling is a practice many large families engage in, and Campbells are no exception. While excellent records remain from the beginning of the farm and brewery, oral depictions are repeated to keep the deceased ancestor's lives meaningful and relevant. Funny stories of events at the farm or brewery over the years are also shared, mostly by Rooster. His stories, filled with laughter and nostalgia, have a way of bringing the family's history to life.

It was late on a Thursday afternoon when Chuck stopped by the Pump House to meet Brooks and Bobby and have them sign some legal documents. Rooster came in later to share a drink. During a conversation on current events involving a fatal automobile accident the previous day at a nearby intersection, Rooster mentioned that the deceased had the last name Walker. After extinguishing the sad details of the young man's passing, Rooster said the name Walker reminded him of a young sharecropping couple who lived at the farm in the late 50s. According to Rooster, Sir Walker, as he was called, came in from the field one day, earlier than expected, and found his young bride on the bottom side of another man. Walker was speechless and slowly turned to walk away. The young

Cassanova wasted no time grabbing his clothes and jumped from the window, expecting a shotgun blast at any moment. As he ran away, Walker lowered an H&R single shot 16 gauge on his target and unloaded a healthy dose of #8 birdshot across the philanderer's naked backside, and the yell that followed could be heard a mile away.

Rooster said at the hearing regarding the shooting, the judge asked Walker to describe what he had seen on the date in question. Walker replied, "Well, ya see judge, I come in from the field expecting some pork, greens, and cornbread, but instead sees them two fuckin'." The half-asleep judge banged his gavel and huffed at Walker's comment. He scowled and said, "Young man, I'll have none of that language in my courtroom.

Walker slumped and apologized. The judge repeated the question, and Walker replied similarly, "I come in from the field hungry and looking to eat, and they in there fuckin'." The judge threw his hands up and sternly warned Walker of his infraction and promised to fine five dollars should it happen again.

"Now," the judge said, "For the third time, please describe in detail the events you witnessed on such and such date without using profanity."

Walker looked ahead and said, "I got off from working in the fields on Mr. Asa Campbell's farm. I go into my house expecting to eat but instead, I see ten toes up and ten toes down. Two big asses going round and round. A big black root going out and in, and if that ain't fuckin', you can fine me ten!" While the boys had undoubtedly heard this tale a few times, it was Chuck's first, and he nearly choked on his beer.

When Brooks and Chuck were children in the early 80s, they rode on the Campbell Farm for miles on bicycles or motorcycles and often stopped by the Pump House, which was open for business in those days.

They pitted in one hot July afternoon for a quick break to enjoy a cold Coke. In those days, a fellow named Gus Durant ran the station for the Campbells. Gus was pleasant enough but did enjoy his vodka, and he didn't let working get in the way of his afternoon snorts.

While not on the main stretch of the highway, the store would get the occasional out-of-towner looking for a reprieve or a full tank. One day, a lady stopped in, driving a new Cadillac. She asked for a fill-up and to use the restroom facilities. Mr. Durant pointed to the corner restroom and went outside to pump her gas. The hot, dusty wind swirled as he whistled an old tune, his hands moving methodically as he worked, seemingly lost in the rhythm of the task.

Once the traveler emerged from inside, she pointed to a weathered, metal Coca-Cola sign that read "Enjoy Coke and Clean Restrooms." She said, "Sir, I'll have you know, that restroom is not what I call clean!"

Durant said, "My apologies, madam." A bead of sweat ran down his temple, but he wiped it away with his sleeve, keeping his cool. "I'll deal with that right away," and after pumping her gas, he hopped in his 67 Dodge pickup and backed over the sign, leaving it in a crumpled state, dragged by his truck as he sailed back to his parking spot. The sound of metal scraping against gravel echoed through the lot, catching the attention of the boys and a few onlookers who stood in disbelief.

Walking back toward the station, he said, "Now what does the damn sign say?" The lady, with both arms across her chest and mouth agape, as if she'd witnessed an alien craft landing among the pecan trees, said, "Well, I never!" and hurried along her way.

# Chapter 5

By the time the United States entered Prohibition in January of 1920, Karl Schneider had retired due to poor health. Still, with Young and Campbell's leadership, the Brewery and import whisky business had grown quite lucrative. While the men detested the move by the government, they had no choice but to comply, shut down, and furloughed most of their brewery workforce. By this time, with the money saved and the farm income, the family had more than enough to see them through. Unfortunately, the Grange Distillery in Scotland didn't fare so well. With over 90% of their sales going to the United States and Canada, they soon shuttered their doors and closed forever.

Before the 20s, the farm grew barley during the winter and cotton during the summer. The brewery used barley, and the farm sold the cotton as a cash crop. Cotton was high at the beginning of the 1920s, reaching almost $.40 per pound; however, the price had fallen to the single digits by the decade's end. In addition to low prices, another blow to the Campbell Farm and hundreds of other southern farmers was the Bol Weevil's arrival in 1919. Asa Campbell would often say in later years, "Between the goddamn government and the boll weevil, I was getting fucked at both ends. We didn't pick enough cotton some years to make a pygmy's dress."

The Depression of 1929 got all the attention, but it hit earlier for farmers across the South. To add to the misery, a three-year drought beginning in 1925 stressed an already anemic farming economy, and many farms, along with their creditors, failed. The Thronateeska got so low in 1926 that families near the river planted peas and corn crops in the riverbed just to survive. When people talk about "The Good 'Ol Days," I assume they aren't talking about these.

Although prohibition certainly made alcohol illegal, miraculously, it didn't diminish the desire of Americans to suckle from the nectar of the gods. Although the brewery was closed for business, it never actually ceased brewing beer. While certainly not in volumes before, the family and locals couldn't be expected to quit cold turkey.

Remembering his time at the Grange Distillery, Asa constructed a still out of a couple of sheets of copper. He placed it on the banks of the river, using the cold water from a blue hole to condense the vapors. Before long, Asa was bottling 90-proof moonshine. While there was undoubtedly a market for his product, Young instructed him not to sell but to store the shine and wait until called for. The truth of the matter was the elder Young needed to get a finger on the pulse of the politics of illegal whisky.

By the 1920s, The Schneider, Young, and Campbell families were well-known and largely respected community members. The brewery employed over 50 men and had a reputation for being some of the best-paying work in the area. Of course, they had their detractors. Several clergy members and busy-body church folk were a constant source of criticism and judgment. This was, in fact, the family who made the Devil's brew!

A.P. McWaters had been the sheriff of Sullivan County for over twenty years and was thought by most to be fair and decent. He was a man of few words, known for his steady hand and pragmatic approach to the law, solving disputes with calm reasoning rather than force.

When Young and Campbell met with McWaters, he informed the two there wasn't a state or county law prohibiting alcohol, so he didn't plan on spending one second of his or his deputies' time enforcing the rules of "The Great Experiment."

While much has been made in movies and television about the heavy-handed implementation of prohibition laws, the illegal production of wine, beer, and spirits was often overlooked. In reality, small operations flourished, with most local law enforcement turning a blind eye, especially in rural areas like Sullivan County, where people largely kept to themselves.

US Marshalls initially carried out enforcement and later became agents of the Treasury Department, but underfunding, meager training, and even corruption were commonplace. The bureaucratic red tape and under-the-table deals ensured that many illegal distillers operated with little fear of serious reprisal, especially in the remote southern counties.

So, a law designed to enforce morality and social progress became the genesis of modern human history's most significant crime opportunity. While no one in Sullivan County was looking to become an Al Capone, any shrewd businessman would be negligent in letting a moderate-risk and high-reward opportunity pass. It was only a short time before Young and Campbell had the details ironed out and began moving Asa's product down the Thronateeska to Apalachicola, Florid

# Chapter 6

Today, the Schneider Brewery employs 135 full-time employees, with 35 exceeding 20 years of tenure. Although Brooks has an office at the brewery, Bobby is the Campbell in charge, and all decisions go through him, which is just fine with little brother, who would rather be in the fields on a tractor or working with the cows than cooped up in an office. Bobby's son, Joe, works as a junior brewmaster at Schneider. Libby Maddox, an industry expert, primarily manages day-to-day operations. John and Bobby recruited Libby from one of the larger breweries several years ago.

For years, the family's brewery has been a target of acquisition from the big brands. Although several offers have been made, they have all been flatly yet politely declined. Despite the allure of big money, they remain committed to maintaining control over their operations and heritage. While hops and rice are shipped in, half of the barley used by the brewery is grown on the Campbell Farm, and much of the by-products are used as livestock feed for the cattle operation.

Brooks manages the farm, which includes a beef processing facility. A few years back, the Campbell men traveled to Argentina for a week of dove hunting. While there, they visited some local cattle ranches and were impressed by how the animals were raised and prepared for slaughter. In the US, cattle are typically sold as weaned calves and then moved to compact feedlots, where they are taken off grass and fed grains until slaughter.

In Argentina, the group observed the animals being left on grass for much longer, with supplemental feed added a few months before processing. Tasting the difference firsthand, the Campbells were struck by the richness and depth of flavor in the Argentine beef—a marked contrast to what they had grown accustomed to back home. Inspired by this experience, they decided to implement similar methods on their farm.

Upon their return, they began constructing the processing facility. After inspection and certification by the USDA, the plant was soon up and running. They process the cattle not only from their farm but local ranches as well. The facility is run by an Argentinian immigrant, Carlos Coria, known to the family as CC. The beef is sold in a few local grocery stores and at Campbell's Farm Store next to the Vet Hospital.

In addition to the farm, the family owns a 3-acre estate in the Bahamas. The beachfront location has been a gathering place for family and friends for over 30 years. John, Madie and Clover purchased the land decades ago, drawn to the island's pristine beauty and the promise of creating a sanctuary far removed from the demands of their everyday lives. Over the years, they transformed the parcel into a four-bedroom haven, a place where family ties are strengthened and memories are made. The house, nestled between palm trees and white sand, stands as a testament to their love for the island and for one another. It has become a second home – a place where the sounds of laughter mingle with the rhythmic crash of waves and where life slows to the natural pace of the Caribbean tides. Every visit begins with a familiar ritual: a flight aboard the family's 1989 Cessna Grand Caravan, expertly piloted by Alex, a Fed-Ex Pilot. The flight itself has become part of the magic, with family members leaning over to watch the sparkling turquoise waters unfold below as they approach the island. At the marina, a 42-foot Yellow Fin Center Console, jointly owned by Alex, Bobby, and Brooks, waits to ferry them into the deeper, quieter reaches of the Caribbean, where adventure and solitude blend effortlessly. Docked alongside sleek yachts, the boat is a symbol of the Campbells' deep connection to the sea, a vital part of their island life.

A Campbell Family tradition involves celebrating Thanksgiving each year in the Bahamas, where they gather at the island home to feast on fresh-caught local seafood – snapper, conch and lobster – paired with dishes that have graced their table for decades. The holiday isn't just a meal; it's a time when the bonds of family are renewed, stories are shared, and the natural beauty of the Caribbean becomes the backdrop to their laughter and love. As the golden sunsets over the ocean, painting the sky in brilliant hues of pink and orange, the Campbells know they are part of something bigger than themselves—a legacy of family that stretches across land and sea.

Chuck travels with his two sons each winter to the island with Brooks, Bobby, Joe, Jake, and Alex on a yearly fishing excursion. Just like Chuck, Bobby, and Brooks, the boys have known each other since birth and are very close friends.

While Dottie's daughter, Jenna, doesn't attend the yearly fishing trip, she's as close to Chuck's boys as her cousins are. His oldest, Andrew (Andy), and Jenna have been sweethearts since high school. Andy finally popped the question, and the two married a few years back.

It would be an understatement to say Chuck's wife Chanda and Dottie were consumed with this wedding. Alex and Chuck could hardly walk through the door of their respective homes without some new honey-do list cast upon them. Almost causing a divorce, Alex suggested the two elope and take the money he and Dottie plan to spend on the nuptials. Dottie scolded Alex as if he'd told the two youngsters to carry out a Thelma and Louise leap off a cliff. Even Chuck was placed in the doghouse for Alex's transgression, with his wife insinuating the two were scheming against them in hopes of getting out of the work and money involved.

A few weeks before the wedding, Chuck met Alex, Bobby, and Brooks at the Pump House. Alex was returning from Albany airport wearing his Fed-Ex Captain's uniform. At the time, Alex was deadheading from Albany and Atlanta before reaching Detroit, where he commanded the controls of an Airbus A300 en route to Hong Kong. His usually sharp appearance was worn down by exhaustion, the dark circles under his eyes betraying the toll of endless flights and pre-wedding stress. He was looking especially haggard from this trip.

Brooks asked, "Damn brother-in-law, you didn't catch that Asian Flu in Hong Kong, did ya?"

He replied, "Naw, I don't think so, but hell, I could use a few days of convalescence if it would give me some peace from your sister's nagging about this wedding. You boys have no idea how off-the-chain Dorothy has become." He slumped back in the chair, rubbing his forehead with a mix of frustration and affection. It was clear he loved Dottie, but the wedding preparation was testing every ounce of his patience. Bobby and Brooks both looked at each other with raised eyebrows.

Brooks said, "Trust me- We know! Don't you remember when Mom and Dad had their 50th wedding anniversary? You would have thought she was planning a visit from the Queen." His voice held a hint of playful exasperation, but the memory seemed to spark a warmth in his expression, a fondness for Dottie's meticulous ways. Alex nodded in agreement as Rooster walked in with his German Sheppard, Prince.

Bobby said, "Well, if it ain't Prince and the Revolution, Do pull up a chair, fellas." Rooster found a seat while Prince greeted Bobby's Pointer, John Henry, and Brooks' Scottie, Hank, and border collie, Pearl.

Rooster heard the last part of the conversation and chimed in. "Now Alex, surely you know how mamas feel about their daughters getting hitched. Shit boy, that's y'all's only child, and a girl to boot. Little Dottie will make damn sure it's perfect, or as perfect as humanly possible. Weddings are like cocaine to women folk. Hell, you know, even Sweet asked me not too long ago if I wanted to renew my vows. I said hell no! I told you I loved you when I married ya back in '65. If I change my mind, I'll let you know." They all laughed at Rooster's bit of enlightenment. His gruff humor always had a way of easing the tension, pulling laughter from the most worn-out souls in the room.

Brooks told Alex and Chuck, "You will live through this; just do as you're told and don't, under any circumstances, offer suggestions or advice, even if asked for." Rooster and Bobby nodded in agreement. The dogs ambled outside the back screen door, which Prince had learned to open for his brethren some time ago. They ran into the orchard, chasing a couple of thieving squirrels. The men followed, settling on the back porch. The cool evening air felt like a balm after the stifling heat of the day, and the rhythmic barking of the dogs added a sense of normalcy to the otherwise hectic lives of these men.

John Campbell pulled up in his father's 1963 Ford F-100 with his border collie, Jack. The two exited the truck, and Jack joined his K-9 cousins in the orchard while John settled in a rocker by Rooster. He said, "Roost, you keeping these shitheads straight?"

"Gave up long ago," he declared.

John asked Alex, "How's my favorite wedding planner today?" Alex looked at his father-in-law with a hopeless expression as if to beg for rescue from his current despair but instead replied sarcastically, "Oh Pop, it's absolutely a thrilling and rewarding experience. Who wouldn't relish the opportunity to prepare for the day their daughter becomes a Langdon?" His voice dripped with sarcasm, but underneath, there was a thread of pride. Despite the complaints, Alex was every bit the doting father, ready to walk his daughter down the aisle.

John laughed and said, "Aww boy, you'll survive. Shit, just roll with it.",

"It's been too long since we've had a good old-fashioned wedding on this farm. I'm sure it will be one helluva party, and I'm happy for Jenna and Andy." He looked at Chuck and Alex with a more serious expression, "This ain't about y'all, it's about these kids, so suck it up and quit your bitchin', both of ya!" Mr. John has always served as a second father to Chuck and Alex and is quick to offer a clear voice of admonishment when needed, just as soon as he would his sons.

The elder Campbell asked Rooster if he'd seen Vic Reynolds lately. Rooster replied in the negative. John crossed his hands behind his head and leaned back in the rocker, "Well, he came to the hospital the other day to have Clover look at that sissy ass dog he's always sportin' around town with." John looked around at the others to ensure they were listening and continued, "You know his momma died a couple of months back. According to my sister, he's come from the corner, as they say." Rooster, along with Bobby, Alex, and Chuck, looked at John, puzzled. However, Brooks caught his dad's verbal misstep and let out a huge belly laugh, bending over and grabbing behind his knees. The others looked at him confusedly as he rose, catching his breath. He said, "Daddy, don't you mean to say he's come out of the closet?" John pointed at Brooks, shaking his hand, and said, "Yeah, yeah, that's it. What did I say?" The rest of the group let out similar outbursts of laughter as Brooks had earlier displayed, and he said, "Oh Daddy, that shit is just perfect, and that's what I'll call it from now on, Coming from the Corner."

Rooster chuckled and said, "Well, I don't know if it was a real secret to anyone who knew that boy, except maybe his mama. Everybody knows he got some sugar in his tank, always has." Brooks said, "Hell yeah, but 'old Vic's alright. He can play the hell out of a piano, and we love him like family. Hell, he's like a gay uncle."

John said, "Oh yeah, he and Clover have always been good buddies, even back in school. I tell you what, he's one funny joker too! Y'all remember, after your mother died, how the three of us went to Scotland for a couple of weeks?" They all acknowledged the memory, and he continued. "Vic made that trip a lot of fun. It was just what I needed. You know, one night, Clover turned in early, and Vic and I went looking for a pub to down a couple of pints. We happened upon a place called the "Silver Tassie." As luck would have it, it was karaoke night, and we settled in at the bar with the locals. Although they were using a D.J., they had instruments. Vic requested Elvis' "Suspicious Minds." When our time came, we asked if we could use the guitar and keyboards. Vic took the piano, and I grabbed the guitar. The locals loved it, and we went back the next two nights with Clover joining us. We sang a few more numbers but mostly played backup for the local talent. We had so much fun. I can only say I felt as though I had been a local for years. Maybe it's my Scottish roots, but I felt like I was at home."

The trip to Scotland following Madie's death was a needed retreat for John and Clover. Vic owned a travel agency in Albany years ago and, still today, sees himself as an expert in all things travel-related. Vic pitched the idea to Clover, and she bought in, purchasing John's ticket and all travel-related expenses. The kids became involved and ensured their dad didn't plan anything for the two weeks they would be gone.

The family planned a Saturday barbecue at the lake house the week before departure. Before everyone ate, Vic and Clover stood in front of the crowd and gathered everyone's attention. Vic, acting as MC, pulled an envelope from the inside pocket of his linen blazer, looked at the group, and said, "Before we eat, I'd just like to say how much I love this family. I know you have all been dealt a heavy blow with the untimely passing of your sweet mother and John's beloved Madie. A couple of weeks ago, I suggested to Clover that it would be a nice distraction for John to get away for a few days, so in this envelope, I have three first-class tickets for John, Clover, and myself to Edinburgh, Scotland."

Vic looked at John's expression of surprise and continued, "John, before you try and wiggle out of this, just know all your children, grandchildren, as well as Rooster and Sweet are in on this surprise, so we'll hogtie you if we must and place you on that plane next Saturday." The crowd laughed, cheered, and applauded.

Dottie walked up to her dad, grabbed his hands, and said, "Daddy, we all think this would be good for you, so please just go with it and have a ball."

Although not as excited as the rest of the party, John agreed. As they all fixed their plates and found a seat, Clover and Vic arranged themselves on each side of John, acquainting him with the itinerary. Later that evening, Rooster built a fire in the outdoor fireplace. Bobby and Brooks played a few tunes on guitar and harmonica, and Dottie sang one of John's favorites, "I Was Raised on Country Sunshine" by Dottie West.

# Chapter 7

Once the decision to move the shine downriver to Apalachicola, a sturdy but disposable river barge was constructed to make the trip, and soon, Asa and Dock Smith were headed south at a leisurely pace. Dock was a black sharecropper who lived on the farm and helped Asa build the still. Asa brought a copy of Mark Twain's Huckleberry Finn on the trip and read it aloud to Dock. When the two arrived in Apalachicola, Asa jokingly referred to Dock as "Jim." Dock had chuckled at the comparison, though there was a shared understanding of the deeper complexities of race and friendship in the South that went unspoken between them.

In Apalachicola, a receiver named Joe Starling met the two and their cargo. The process for which prior communication with Starling occurred was in the form of sending a simple postcard with the message, "The sow had her piglets." Starling would then reply with the date to have the shipment sent.

Asa had never met Starling and was understandably apprehensive as their journey ended. The quiet tension in the air as they docked was palpable; Asa wasn't sure whether Starling was the kind of man who could be trusted, especially given the nature of their business. However, after meeting him, he was relieved. Asa said in later years as he was recounting the story, "Joe Starling looked exactly like Otis from the Andy Griffith Show and was just about as drunk."

The portly Starling surveyed the shipment and sampled a few bottles to ensure he wasn't buying spring water. As he took a swig from the last bottle, he said, "Damn, mighty fine boy! Looks like you folks up there can make bout as good hooch as you do beer!"

Once the shine was in Starling's possession, it was moved to various locations along the FL Panhandle and the state's lower peninsula, distributed to buyers along the way. This arrangement continued for the next ten years, providing a nice supplemental income for the Campbell and Young families.

Roosevelt signed the Cullen-Harrison Act in the spring of 1933, making alcohol legal again. The state of Georgia followed and by 1935, the Schneider Brewery was back in business, albeit operating under different practices than before.

Before prohibition, breweries were allowed to sell their products directly, with the larger breweries owning bars and saloons. However, the new law prohibited this practice and required manufacturers to sell to wholesalers, who then managed the distribution to retail outlets.

The new format was challenging, and revenues decreased initially from where they had been before 1920. Several American breweries didn't survive, but the Schneider brand had a loyal following. It endured and expanded operations. As the 1930s progressed, the brewery exceeded pre-prohibition sales and showed a healthy profit despite the economic woes of the Depression.

# Chapter 8

**A**lthough the brewery was successful, Asa and Katie were battling personal struggles with the health of their daughter Cora, who was diagnosed with leukemia in the summer of 1934. The child lasted only four months after becoming ill and passed away in December of the same year. The loss shattered Asa and Katie. Their grief ran deep, lingering in every corner of their once joyful home. They mourned not only for the daughter they lost but for the life she would never live. Each day felt heavier than the last, their sorrow intertwining with every aspect of their lives as they struggled to cope with a world forever changed by her absence.

A second blow occurred just ten years later when they received word that their son Thomas had been killed in action in Belgium in December of 1944.

Losing one child is tragic, but losing all your children is pure hell on earth. The grief was suffocating, threatening to break them in ways they never imagined. Yet, while such loss often drives couples apart, Asa and Katie clung to each other for dear life, desperate for any sense of comfort.

That winter, they stayed in bed for days, their arms wrapped tightly around one another, holding on as if letting go would mean losing everything. They wept together, their cries echoing through the walls, not just for the children they had lost but for the unanswered questions that haunted their souls. In their darkest moments, they turned to God, pleading for reasons, for meaning, for something to ease the ache in their hearts.

Henry Hubert and his wife Betty came daily to prepare food and check in with the grieving couple. They often wondered if they would find them alive or dead, unaware if they had the strength to overcome. As a precaution, Henry removed all the firearms from the house without Asa knowing. Katie's parents passed away in the late 1930s, so Henry and Betty were the only "family" they had.

In February of 1945, Katie was awakened by what she thought was a dream. The night had been still, but her heart pounded as if she'd run a great distance. She bolted up and, taking a moment to gather her senses, found herself drenched in sweat. Her nightgown clung to her skin, but she wasn't cold. The warmth she felt wasn't from the blankets or Asa's presence – it radiated from within, as though her very soul had been touched. She didn't feel feverish or ill; quite the contrary, she felt exuberant.

Was it a dream? Katie thought. It seemed so natural and real as she looked at Asa sleeping peacefully beside her. His steady breathing was a stark contrast to the whirlwind of emotions inside her. She reached out to touch his hand, finding comfort in his presence, but something urged her to listen more closely. There it was again -the sweetest voice filled her ears, giving her a sense of peace and hope never experienced before. It was as though heaven itself whispered to her a reassurance she had longed for since

Thomas' passing. Katie woke Asa up, telling him God told her she would be a mother again.

Asa, half asleep, looked at his wife with a slight smile but a perplexed stare. The fog of sleep clung to him, and he blinked slowly, trying to make sense of her words. Katie continued, ignoring her husband's look of confusion. She told Asa they were to go to the riverbank where they first made love all those years ago, and God would bless them with another child. Her voice carried an unmistakable conviction, something deeper than just hopes – it was certainty. Asa, now more awake, listened carefully, though still struggling to grasp it all.

The next day was mild and sunny, so Katie prepared lunch, and they rode horseback to the banks of the Thronateeska. The gentle breeze seemed to carry the scent of spring, even though winter hadn't quite loosened its grip on the land. The ride was quiet, but not in the usual way. It was filled with unspoken anticipation.

Katie laid a quilt by the riverbank, and the two made love for the first time in months. The act wasn't just physical; it felt like a return to life, as though something long dormant had been awakened within them. Each touch was a rediscovery, a reminder of the love they had always shared but had buried beneath layers of sorrow.

They had allowed grief to consume their lives for so long that they forgot how much they enjoyed giving themselves to each other. Their eyes were locked in loving gazes of passion, each appreciating the same, yet faint, youthful freckles they fell in love with in Scotland. At that moment, time seemed to fold in on itself, and they were no longer the weary couple who had endured so much pain but the young lovers who had once believed anything was possible. Asa laid his chest on Katie's bare breast for several minutes as she stroked his hair, and at that moment, she knew God had fulfilled his promise.

After lunch, the two took a track north and stopped by the brewery. The familiar scent of barley and hops wafted through the air as they approached, bringing with it memories of a time when life had been simpler. When they entered the offices, Clara Bell Smith, Asa's secretary, greeted them warmly and was delighted to see them with an upbeat demeanor.

The two stayed for a few hours and returned home late afternoon. As they approached home, the sunset showed a splendid display behind the barn where the horses were stabled. After dismounting and removing their saddles, they walked to the fenced lot behind the barn, leaned on the cedar fence bracing, and enjoyed the dancing of colors. The sky was ablaze with oranges, pinks, and purples, a canvas painted by a hand greater than their own, and it felt as if the heavens were speaking directly to them.

Asa took Katie in his arms and said, "Katie, God didn't speak to me last night, but I know he put us together and has a purpose for our lives, and I'm counting this sunset we've caught together as a sign of his promise to you last night." Katie leaned her head on his shoulder, tears welling in her eyes – not from sadness, but from a deep, overwhelming gratitude. In that sunset, she saw not just a promise but a future filled with hope.

As Spring arrived and settled in 1945, Katie and Asa were not surprised to learn that Katie was indeed pregnant. She and Asa were glowing from the excitement and anticipation of being parents again.

Katie's doctor thought he heard two heartbeats in late August, so he ordered an x-ray of her abdomen to verify, and sure enough, there were two babies! Due to her age and some mild spotting, he called for strict bedrest for the remainder of the pregnancy.

Betty Hubert all but moved in, caring for Katie, and she, Henry, and young Herny III (Rooster) ate with the family each night. As Katie entered her ninth month, Asa put up a cedar tree in the front parlor room, and Betty decorated the home for the babies' first Christmas with holly clippings and red bows.

On December 16, 1945, Katie entered labor in the early morning hours. Asa summoned the doctor, and the twins were delivered at sunrise without issue. Christmas was a happy time for the family, farm, and brewery employees. Asa ordered cigars for all the men at the brewery and gave each employee a Christmas bonus of $50.

# Chapter 9

In June a few years ago, the week finally arrived when Andy and Jenna were to be married. The bride and groom chose to have their ceremony on the banks of the Thronateeska on the grounds of the lake lodge. A 40-by-60-foot tent was erected, its towering white peaks standing out against the lush landscape. Inside, a spacious dance floor gleamed under soft lights, while a stage dominated at the north end.

The air buzzed with anticipation, carrying the faint scent of magnolia blossoms that filled the space. Each guest's table was draped in white tablecloths accented by magnolia blossoms and Blue Willow place settings, leaf clippings, and framed photos of the couple from childhood to the present. Bouquets of magnolia blooms and glossy leaves adorned the serving tables, their fragrance subtly mingling with the aromas of the soon-to-be-served feast, while upright whiskey barrels dotted the space. Adding a rustic touch to the otherwise sophisticated atmosphere. Jenna even decided on a simple yet elegant bridal display of magnolias with pink roses added for color.

As Vic played on the keyboard the old familiar wedding march, Jenna was escorted down the aisle by her father, Alex. Jenna altered her grandmother Madie's dress in the "Grandmillennial" style for the wedding.

Dottie looked on with a sense of pride not experienced before, and when her daughter glanced her way, she silently mouthed "I Love You" to her baby girl, which she returned with a blown kiss.

None of the Campbells were church members, so Rooster officiated the wedding. Rooster was ordained in the early 80s when he served as the interim pastor of the Spring Creek Congregational Methodist Church.

After the ceremony, the family and guests dined on prime rib, brisket tacos and sliders with white and traditional tangy barbecue sauce. The menu comprised sides of creamy coleslaw with pickled onions, red-skinned potato salad, and Brunswick Stew. A three-layer wedding cake, groom's cake, pecan, and sweet potato pies completed the spread. Sweet tea and a well-stocked bar of spirits, Schneider Beer and Schlight, were offered.

A popular local band, "The Thronateeska Cowboys," covered music for the wedding. The newly married couple spent their first night at Clover's home, which she had offered them for as long as needed. The following day, they headed to Atlanta for a flight to Portugal for their honeymoon.

Both sets of the couple's parents, along with Brooks, Amy, Bobby, Julie, Joe, Jake, and Chuck's youngest, Billy, stayed overnight at the lodge the night of the wedding.

After breakfast and tidying up a bit Sunday morning, the group decided to load up the boats and headed to the Sandbar for some relaxation. Brooks loaded all the leftover beer from the wedding to share with the Sandbar Cartel, and they headed out.

Upon arrival, they anchored among 15-20 boats already in place. The day was uniquely relaxing; having got the wedding behind them, they enjoyed a few hours of fellowship with the sandbar regulars.

Before joining the family at the sandbar, the boys took a detour to the blue hole near the state park. This particular blue hole is one of the more popular due to its size. The location is somewhat hidden and easily missed if one isn't familiar with the site. Only a narrow water channel connects the cove, winding through multiple cypress trees and opening to a two-acre body of clear and cold water. On the south end, an outcropping of limestone rock emerges from the bank, offering boaters a convenient place to anchor and use as a platform for jumping into the water. Nearby, a tall Magnolia tree hosts a rope swing from one of its branches, which the kids use to sail into the cold water.

The location is quite popular with teenagers and adults but has some risks. Last summer, a teenage boy and a friend from Atlanta were visiting his grandparents, who lived on the lake. The teen swung out, entering the water, but didn't resurface. A local firefighter and paramedic happened to be onsite that day and quickly dove in. However, once located, he couldn't be revived. Although a good swimmer, the shock of the cold water triggered involuntary inhalation, filling his lungs with water. Following the tragedy, the swimming area was closed for the next few weeks, and the Georgia Department of Natural Resources placed a warning sign to would-be swimmers before reopening.

While John and Clover rarely join the younger Campbells on boating excursions to the sandbar, they often take the pontoon out with their dogs. Both enjoy a leisurely cruise, especially at sunset.

Sunset cruises were also one of John and Madie's favorite pastimes. Madie was a hobby photographer and loved capturing the lake's wildlife. John often asked his wife, "Hey, Madie-Bird, you wanna go chase some sunsets and have a cocktail on the river?"

Lake Early's upper section's western shore truly offers spectacular sundown views. The reds, ambers, and pinks trace the silhouettes of wispy clouds, setting a fiery backdrop for cypress trees cloaked in Spanish moss in the lake's backwaters, offering a glimpse of what heaven must eternally look like.

# Chapter 10

**C**lover still owns the 68 Lincoln she drove from San Diego following Ray's death. It has been exceptionally well maintained with cranberry paint and is near showroom condition. While it's not Clover's daily driver, she takes it out at least once a week to stretch its legs. The older Lincoln is a favorite of her nephews, each borrowing it occasionally for special occasions or date nights. In addition to the 68 Lincoln, a few other antique vehicles are still used around the farm. John still occasionally drives his father's 63 F100, and a 1938 Dodge 1-½ ton flatbed truck is kept at the brewery and used for company promotions and holiday parades locally.

Another prized vehicle is the family's Blue Bird Wanderlodge motor home, manufactured in 1978 just up the road in Fort Valley, Georgia. John purchased the RV for weekend trips to the Georgia mountains.

In April of 1981, the family took it out west on a two-week vacation. The trip out west was the first for the Campbell children. At the time, their ages were 14,12 and 7. John and Madie planned the trip for months around the kids' week-long spring break from school. They had poured over maps, excitedly discussing stops and sights, sharing their own childhood memories of road trips, and imagining the wonder their kids would feel seeing these places for the first time. Neither John nor Madie were ever sticklers for perfect school attendance, so missing a week from school wasn't stressed over.

The family of five and their Scottie, Riley, left the farm on April 4, 1981. The early spring air was crisp, and as they waved goodbye to the familiar fields and barns, a sense of freedom settled in – a break from the routine of the farm and brewery. John loosened the harness on the "Bird" as he merged into traffic on Interstate 75. The big Caterpillar V8 hummed, never missing a lick, and in three days, John had the Bird at the Grand Canyon's south rim. The kids, usually full of chatter, stood in silent wonder as they gazed at the canyon's edge, the sheer size of it beyond anything they'd imagined.

Next, they ventured to the towering sequoias of Yosemite, where John shared stories of his youth and the times he and Madie had wandered these same trails before they had children. Their voices echoed softly through the forest as they pointed out the grandeur of the trees, feeling small but connected to the majesty of nature.

One of the most meaningful stops for John was Edwards Air Force Base, where he had been stationed during the Vietnam War. As they drove through the base, John's face softened with nostalgia, memories of his younger self flashing through his mind. He shared tales of the days he spent there, the missions, the camaraderie, and meeting his sweet Madie. Madie squeezed his hand and gave him a mischievous smile as she recalled their early courtship days in California.

John joined the Air Force Reserves in the spring of his junior year in high school. He completed his basic training during his summer break and stayed in the reserves for eight years. Like many reservists, he was called to active duty during the Vietnam War. He completed all two years of active duty at Edwards in California. John and Madie made plans to return to Edwards to see the first landing of the Space Shuttle Columbia, joining hundreds of other RVs.

Over 400,000 visitors lined up on a dry lakebed to watch the Columbia's return. John Campbell says to this day; it was the most patriotic and American thing he'd ever seen. Young and old from all over the country waved flags showing national pride, grilling burgers and hotdogs with strangers only a day before. Music played from boom boxes on top of RVs, cars, and pickups.

As the shuttle appeared in the distance, Neal Diamond's, "America", played overhead, giving hundreds of thousands of onlookers' chills. When the shuttle approached the landing strip, Madie captured a great photo of her three children standing on the Bird's roof. Bobby and Brooks were in jeans and flannel shirts, and Dottie wore overalls with a white long sleeved turtleneck with a messy bun tied by a blue bandana. All three waved flags and excitedly jumped up and down as the shuttle passed by.

John filmed the entire scene on Super 8 film and a Kodak camera for the kids to share with their classmates when they returned. Bobby and Dottie were already dreading the essays they had to write on the trip home. Madie and the kids' teachers thought giving them an assignment for the missing week of school would be a good idea. Much groaning came from the kids, but after John said they could always stay home with Aunt Clover, they got in line.

# Chapter 11

**G**eorgia's Lake Early State Park is a popular waterfront destination for locals and visitors. The park offers campsites, cabins, a lakefront beach, a marina, a restaurant, and a 18 hole golf course. The park hosts a barbecue competition each spring, with Schneider Brewery serving as the primary sponsor. The Campbells don't compete in the competition but always attend. Last spring, Bobby parked the Bird at the park as a convenient place to gather. Due to the many visitors stopping by, the holding tanks on the RV became full and needed to be emptied.

A transfer tank on wheels is kept in a storage bay on the Bird, so Brooks transferred the tanks to the portable tank called the "turd hearse." The portable tank has a handle for pulling the contents to a disposal location. However, the nearest waste disposal was at the park's exit, so Brooks hooked the handle over the 2" hitch ball at the rear of his F250. Brooks and Chuck slowly headed out and passed by several barbecue participants and campers with baffled expressions. Upon arriving at the cook site of a mutual friend, Steve Andrews, they stopped as he walked up. Steve said, "Anyone else pulling a load of shit with an F250 would seem odd, but with you two clowns, it seems about right."

Brooks replied, "Well damned if I'm gonna drag this load a half mile by hand!"

They visited for several minutes, and by the time they got on the way, Brooks stepped up his speed, apparently forgetting about the tank of excrement in tow. Cresting a hill, the guys were in mid-conversation when suddenly, the blue tank that was supposed to be at the rear appeared out of the front windshield. Brooks said in disbelief, "What the hell's that?"

To which Chuck replied, "That's our shit!" As they looked on helplessly, the tank rolled downhill, picking up speed but staying in the center of the asphalt path. At the bottom of the hill, the road curved to the left, and outside of the curve sat a campsite where a family of campers were sitting around a picnic table enjoying their lunch.

As the hearse approached the campsite, Chuck and Brooks locked eyes with the family around the table and exchanged looks of sheer terror. The diners quickly jumped from the table, seeking refuge from the approaching dirty bomb. It was as if, by design, the tank torpedoed into the center of the family's campsite, knocking over a table holding a camp stove, a plate of hamburgers, and a pitcher of lemonade.

Thankfully, the hearse remained intact and didn't release its contents. The two apologized profusely, assisted the family with the cleanup, and offered them all the barbecue and Schneider Beer they wanted.

By the time they left the site, they all laughed, and the mother and father of the family almost seemed grateful for the experience, telling them they couldn't wait to tell the story when they got back home.

# Chapter 12

In mid-June, harvest time arrives on the farm. The Campbells grow more barley than any farm in the southeast, with 100% used at the brewery. Considering that one barrel of beer requires a bushel of barley malt and that the brewery produces over 250,000 barrels per year, a considerable amount is needed.

In a good year, the farm yields half of the brewery's barley needs, with the other half coming from other local farms. The farm uses two John Deere X-Series combines capable of covering 20 acres per hour and processing enough every hour to fill a semi-truck or two. The massive machines move like giants across the fields, their blades whirring as they harvest the golden barley.

Once the barley is transferred to the trucks, it's taken directly to the brewery, where it's cleaned and stored until ready for malting, a three-step process of steeping (wetting), germinating, and roasting the grain. The harvest can be completed in a week or two if the weather cooperates. Immediately following the barley harvest, the same fields are planted in corn or soybeans for a fall harvest.

In the early days before mechanized machinery, Asa Campbell and his hired men used mules and horses to plant and combine the fields until the late 30s when tractors replaced the animals. It wasn't until the early 50s when Asa purchased his first self-propelled combine, a Massey Harris 26 model, which remains on the farm today in working condition. It's a yearly tradition to leave a few acres at the end of the harvest for John to gather with the old 26, which he's been operating since he was a young teen.

Another tradition, seeming to be taken from Deuteronomy in the Old Testament, is leaving the corners of the fields in grain. While no orphans, widows, or aliens are likely to need it, the practice is consistently followed. Asa Campbell always said, "Maybe the good Lord would give him credit for feeding the birds and squirrels."

John practices a similar method in the ½ acre vegetable garden he plants every spring. After laying out his rows of silver queen and trucker's favorite corn with his father's 1952 International Super-A tractor, he places some dried corn at each corner of the garden. This sacrificial practice prevents the raccoons, crows, and turkeys from digging up the seed once the corn sprouts. He calls it feeding the garden spirits.

While no Campbell has ever been a regular churchgoer, they are spiritually minded. Asa and Katie often felt the local churches looked down on them, and for the most part, they did.

However, despite what the some thought of them, no church in the area has done more to help people in their community than the Campbell Family. Asa and Katie set up an endowment in the 1960s to assist local community members during hard times.

Countless stories exist where families and individuals, white and black, have been impacted by their generosity. The endowment has allowed numerous local kids to attend college, including Rooster and Sally's son, Grady. Today, the trust is managed by Clover, with John, Rooster, and Sally serving as board members.

From the beginning, the Schneider, Young, and Campbell families treated their employees and fellow community members justly. Back in the old days, they paid black men the same as white men, which wasn't always standard practice. While this caused some discontent among other farms, they didn't care. Asa said, "What's right is right, and what's wrong is wrong, and it's wrong to pay a man less due to the color of his skin."

Perhaps it was because all three men were immigrants and had minimal experience with black people in Europe; therefore, they didn't have any racial prejudice that was common in the South.

Black sharecroppers raised families on the farm, and the Campbell and sharecropper kids played together daily. A yearly fall barbeque involved the entire farm and brewery, where the men cooked a couple of hogs and the ladies prepared sides. Black and white enjoying each other's company.

John Campbell tells a story from his childhood regarding some of the hurtful racist practices he observed. As he tells it, Asa, Henry, Rooster, and John went to Albany to pick up supplies in the 38 Dodge truck. They pulled into a service station, and John noticed a woman standing at the "White Only" water fountain, getting a drink. She then walked to her car, retrieved a small lap dog, and carried her to the fountain, allowing the pup to drink.

Several men were sitting in front of the station and didn't bat an eye, as if this scene was as natural as the wind blowing. But for John, it wasn't. He sat there confused, with disbelief swelling inside him.

He says it hit him like a bull calf barreling down on him. He thought, "A dog is good enough, but not these two?"

It was a life-changing moment for the young man. It was as if a veil was lifted, and he saw the world as it was. Later that night, as the weight of what he had witnessed grew unbearable, he came to his father, tears streaming down his face. His chest tight with emotion, he poured out his heart, telling him what he saw. Asa took him in his lap and hugged him tightly. He told Asa how sad he was for Rooster, Sally and Henry. Asa looked at his son and said, "Son, God spoke to you today. That's what this was. This world can often be unjust and even cruel, but we are only judged on how we treat others, and that's why we treat Henry, Sally, and Rooster as family because they are. We are all God's children."

# Chapter 13

**ndy** and Jenna, back from honeymooning, settled in Aunt Clover's house for the time being. Jenna was in her second year of veterinary school at the University of Georgia and covered much of her clinical internships at Clover and Dottie's practice. Andy finished law school and joined the family firm. Andy's the third generation Langdon in the practice started by his grandfather, Joseph Langdon Jr., in 1965. It's a general practice law firm primarily handling real estate transactions, wills and probates, personal injury, and minor criminal defense cases, Andy's favorite. Jenna loves working with her mom and aunt and has a keen interest in large animal medicine, which is welcome news to her uncles, who run a large herd of beef cattle. Bobby and Brooks are able to cover most issues, as Clover and Dottie have taught them the skills for handling most emergencies, but sometimes, you need that expert on site.

The Campbell Animal Hospital is a large and small animal practice with stall facilities for seeing horses and livestock onsite. Jeb McKinley, a Campbell Hospital vet, currently covers most large animal needs. The practice has a mobile vet truck for use in the field, and Dottie will go out if needed. However, she is happy to let Jeb do it, and he's usually glad to get out of the office. When Jenna is working at the hospital, she always accompanies Jeb on calls. Clover and Dottie are focused on small animals, primarily dogs and cats. However, someone will occasionally bring in a rabbit, hamster, or bird, but a practice rule is no reptiles of any kind!

Dottie is a stickler for dog nutrition and proper weight. She says over 80% of the dogs that enter their practice are overweight, much like their owners. A couple of years after the beef processing facility was opened, Dottie started a dog food brand called "Dr. Dottie's K-9 Complete.

She began with beef organ meat from the farm but added turkey and venison later. The meat is coarsely ground and cooked with green beans, beets, carrots, and sweet potatoes, all superfoods, according to Dottie. The various blends are named after family pets. Sadie's Choice is named after Dottie's Scottie, and Daisy's Turkey Dinner is named after Clover's Scottie. She then adds a proprietary blend of minerals, vitamins, and supplements. The food is vacuum sealed and kept frozen until purchase. The final product is sold at the practice and the Campbell's Farm Store, next to the vet's office.

The store sells beef, pork, chicken, produce, canned vegetables, fruits, cheeses, and locally made sweets. A cooler holds numerous soft drinks and, of course, Schneider Beer. The kitchen in the back makes breakfast six days a week and lunch Monday-Friday. Sweet Hubert's niece, Joyce Henderson, runs the kitchen and is nothing short of a local chef celebrity.

Brooks' son Jake and Chuck's son Billy works in the meat department when not in school or busy with sports. The store is decorated like it's from the 1940s. The building has a worn, cozy charm, the kind that pulls you in with its quiet simplicity. Its rustic appeal is unmistakable. Cypress trees were used as columns along the front porch, with rough-sawn cypress boards running vertically from the ground to the roof along the building's exterior. It looks like it's been there forever, just watching the world go by.

Several antique metal tin signs advertise long-ago brands like Double Cola and Bull Durham Tobacco. On the porch, rocking chairs creak with each slow, easy sway as a few older men use the area as an afternoon gathering spot where they attempt to solve all the world's problems. It's the kind of place steeped in history where the past lingers comfortably in the present, like an old friend who refuses to leave.

# Chapter 14

**D**ave Lewinski was a favorite and loved regular who frequented the store. He and his wife, Bernice, were "Yankey transplants" from New York, and his local friends often referred to him as "New York Dave". They moved to Lake Early over 30 years ago when Dave took an engineering job for the Proctor Gamble plant in Albany. By the time he retired, he was head of plant maintenance. John occasionally joked that Dave and Bernice were some of Schneider's best customers. I've heard him say, "Damned if I've ever seen two old folks drink as much beer as those two." Their home on the lake was the closest to the Campbell lake lodge, and the couple often joined John, Madie, and Clover on afternoon sunset cruises.

One November Sunday afternoon, the couple's daughter in California called John Campbell and asked if he'd seen her parents. She informed John she had been trying to reach them since Friday, but neither would answer. She asked if he minded riding to the house and checking on the couple. John agreed, so she shared the front door key code. John was home with Clover when he received the call just after lunch. Clover asked him to get one of the boys or grandboys to go over with him just to be safe.

John stopped by Brook's and found him tinkering with his Jeep Wrangler. They both hopped in John's F150 and headed to the Lewinski's home. The couple's driveway was long and winding, lined with towering long-leaf Georgia pines, and terminated at the front of the lake-side home, a stately two-story Cape Cod with an attached double garage. The Campbell men exited the truck, and John walked to the front door. Brooks peeked into the garage through the windows and noticed two parked cars, Dave's Ford Explorer and Bernice's Mercedes E300. He informed John of the vehicles in the garage and joined him at the front door. John rang the doorbell and knocked but got no response. Brooks tapped in the code, and they opened the door and began calling for the couple. "Dave, Bernice. Are you folks ok? Your daughter asked us to stop by and check on you."

Again, no response, so the two slowly walked in. Even though the couple's daughter asked them to enter the home, both felt they were breaking in. They walked into the living area and saw nothing out of order. However, as they entered the kitchen, they noticed a chair turned over and a cup of coffee spilled on the floor. They continued calling as they searched the rest of the home. After they entered the couple's bedroom, they saw a king-size bed still unmade but nothing else out of order. They inspected the other three bedrooms and found nothing unusual. The men then returned to the kitchen and surveyed the spilled coffee and chair. Both were careful not to touch anything, remembering their training from watching episodes of Forensic Files.

John told Brooks, "Damned if this makes any sense at all. Where the hell could they be?" Brooks suggested they quickly look in the garage, the one place in the home not checked. The garage door was off the kitchen, so the two headed for the door, carefully avoiding the spilled coffee and chair. The garage was several steps down from the kitchen, and as the men stepped into the garage, they faced the passenger side of Bernice's Mercedes. They peered inside but saw nothing of note. As they walked to the front of the car, the view turned horrific. In front of Dave's Explorer was his headless body. John screamed, "Jesus Christ, Son!" By reflex, Brooks reached for the .45 he brought tucked in his jeans. The two men slowly approached the body and noticed the spilled blood on the floor was dried along with the wound. They backed away and headed outside.

Once outside, Brooks kept his father close as they searched the grounds while Brooks dialed 911. Within 30 minutes, the drive was filled with Sullivan County Police Cruisers and an unmarked Yukon driven by Buck McWaters, the fourth-generation Sheriff of Sullivan County. Buck greeted the Campbells, and they retold the same story just relayed to one of his deputies. Buck asked how long they had known the couple, and John replied, "Since they moved here in the 90s, but damned if I can imagine these two having enemies, certainly not bad enough for this." John shared the daughter's number with the sheriff and informed him that he hadn't called her and hated the idea of having to.

Buck said he would handle it and wanted to know if the Lewinski's were church members. John said they attended the Catholic church in Collinsboro. Buck instructed one of his deputies to inform the priest and asked if he would ride over, but he instructed him not to tell anyone of the death. Bernice Lewinski was nowhere to be found and, while not likely the assailant, was considered a person of interest until located.

Buck turned back to the Campbells and asked whom they told about the death. Brooks said he tried to call Bobby but didn't get an answer, and he called Chuck Langdon, the family attorney, and he was on his way. The sheriff asked, "We'll need to start a search party for Bernice as soon as possible. Mind if we use the boat ramp on y'all's property since it's the closest?" John replied, "Absolutely, and we'll help anyway we can." Brooks suddenly remembered and mentioned that his son, Jake, Billy Langdon, and a couple of other boys stayed at the lake lodge last night. Buck asked if he would call and ask them if they saw anything.

Jake and his friends were fishing upriver when Brooks called. He informed the boys to return immediately; there'd been an emergency at the Lewinski's, and the sheriff needed to speak with them. With Jake still on the phone, Brooks asked Buck if they could dock the boat at the Lewinski's since it would be quicker. The sheriff said, "Yeah, that's fine, but along the seawall, not the dock since it hasn't been processed yet."

Jake asked, "Dad, what's wrong?"

Brooks said, "Son, I don't want to tell you over the phone, but it's about as bad as it fucking gets, so just get here and be careful. Pull the boat up along their seawall and tie it up there.

Within ten minutes, the G3 center console was pulling up and quickly tied down. The tension hung in the air like a storm waiting to break, a sense of dread growing stronger with each step the boys took. The four boys walked up to the front of the house where the sheriff was waiting along with Brooks, John, and Chuck. Buck offered some brief pleasantries to the boys and then informed them of the murder. The news hit like a punch in the gut, leaving them wide-eyed and stunned. He then asked if they saw or heard anything unusual last night. All four boys looked at each other and began nodding their heads.

Tyler Wainright, the oldest of the boys, offered to explain. He said they were returning from the farm store with some items for supper around 6:30 and saw a couple parked on the side of Andrews Road, which leads to the Campbell's and Lewinski's. Tyler said the two were on the back tailgate of the truck having sex. The sheriff raised his head just a notch and said, "Is that a fact, on the side of the damn road?"

Tyler nodded and said, "Hell yeah, sheriff, and they didn't care the least little bit that we saw them either. They just stared at us as we drove by, and the girl smiled." The sheriff shook his head and asked if they saw a license plate.

Billy responded this time, "Yes, sir, Kentucky plates." Buck asked if they happened to write them down.

Jake said, "You couldn't read them because the dude's legs were blocking the numbers, but Billy's right; they were Kentucky plates."

Gage Turner, the last boy to offer up, said, "They were in a beat-up dark blue Chevy Colorado, and those two were high as fuck." The teen caught himself and quickly apologized, but Buck brushed it off and asked, "What do you mean, like high on what?"

Gage said, "Well, not weed, I can tell you that! That dude had a wild ass look in his eyes, and the girl was out of it. They both looked like pure white trash. He had a neck tattoo of a snake."

Jake offered, "Yeah, that girl looked like one of them chicken-head whores who hang around the truck stop on 75, and the guy was a meth monkey for sure." The sheriff then asked if they saw the truck again.

They all nodded in unison. Jake said, "When we got to the lodge, we were over by the outdoor kitchen getting ready to cook. We hadn't got the grill hot when they pulled by slowly and continued around the curve out of sight. We waited to see if they would return, but they didn't." The curve that Jake mentioned leads away from the lodge and towards the direction of the Lewinski home and four others along the lake shore before it dead ends at the last two houses along the lake. The sheriff's jaw tightened as he processed their story, his eyes narrowing. Buck McWaters immediately issued a BOLO for a vehicle and a couple matching the description.

Father Patrick O'Neal arrived from Collinsboro and joined the sheriff inside, where he prayed over the remains of Dave Lewinski. Afterward, Buck asked Father O'Neal if he knew the Lewinski's Daughter, Elaine, who had reached out to John Campbell. The priest said he had met all of their children. Dave and Bernice had a Fourth of July party each year at their lake home for the parish members, and their children were often in attendance. Father O'Neal informed Buck they have a daughter and two sons. Both sons are in the Atlanta area, and Elaine lives in California. With a deep sigh, Buck and the priest decided to make the call together, so they called the Lewinski's daughter, Elaine, and informed her of the tragic news.

The sheriff and priest emerged from the home with blank expressions. They exchanged handshakes, and the priest headed back to Collinsboro. Buck rejoined Chuck, John, Brooks, and the boys standing by John's F150, saying he would be in touch if he had any more questions, and said to John, "Old buddy, I ain't ever seen anything like this." John agreed and said he hoped the two in the truck would be found.

Buck said, "You can bet your ass I'm gonna find those two." John, Brooks, Chuck, and the teens exchanged goodbyes with the sheriff and deputies and left the Lewinski property.

# Chapter 15

**A**fter leaving the Lewinski home, John, Brooks, and Chuck drove to the lake lodge to meet with the Georgia DNR, who were en route to launch their boats in search of Bernice. Each called their families to inform them of the terrible news and then called close friends and neighbors to assist in the search for Bernice. The weight of the tragedy was palpable, the dread in their voices unmistakable. Within the hour, the DNR arrived with two boats and soon launched. They searched the lakeshore south of the Lewinski's home, operating under the grim assumption that they were now looking for a body. The air hung heavy with the unspoken fear that this wasn't a rescue but a recovery.

Soon, the Campbell and Langdon families were joined by other local families in the search for Bernice. Two Sullivan County Deputies organized the search and sent the searchers on foot and in vehicles to designated areas. The search was underway by 2:30 in the afternoon and lasted until sunset. The group met at Campbell's lake lodge and agreed to gather again in the morning if needed.

By 7:00 in the evening, word had gotten out to the community regarding Dave's brutal murder and the apparent kidnapping of Bernice, and the Campbell and Langdon phones were constantly ringing from friends requesting details. The Campbell family stayed at the lodge, joined by the Langdons, the Huberts, and Vic Reynolds.

It was clear no one wanted to be alone that night. Though it was mid-November, the evening was mild, in the high 50s. They decided to eat together, so Billy and Jake went to the store to pick up some steaks and sides. Rooster built a fire, its flame flickering as if trying to fend off the darkness settling over the group. As they sat around the fire, John recalled the day's events, starting with the call from Dave and Bernice's daughter and ending with the sheriff arriving. John told the crowd that Brooks could tell what the boys saw because it was below his pay grade.

Brooks described the young couple having sex on the side of the road and mentioned the Kentucky plates. He added the boys' descriptions of the pair and how they appeared high on something. Billy and Jake returned from the store and joined the group.

Bobby asked, "Jake, say that girl looked like one of them chicken head whores, huh?" Jake said, "Yep, she sure did. I tell you what, that guy had a wild ass look in his eyes. When we rode by, that joker never slowed down. He just looked at us with a wild-eyed expression and licked his lips." A hush fell over the group at that detail.

Brooks' eyes narrowed with a curled upper lip and said, "Good God, What a sick son of a bitch!" The group murmured, exchanging glances. It was clear the situation had everyone on edge.

Breaking the tension, Dottie leaned over to Clover and asked, "Did you speak with Mrs. Collier the other day when she came in?"

Clover furrowed her brow, "No, why?"

Dottie replied, "She brought in a young male cat to get neutered and mentioned that her niece was visiting from Kentucky for a few days with her fiancé. I remember her saying she wasn't impressed by the boy and would be glad when they left." Dottie's voice had that knowing tone, the kind people get when they suspect trouble but don't want to say it outright.

Brooks asked, "Did she mention anything else?"

Dottie shook her head, "Not that I can recall, but you could tell she was ready for them to go."

Billy leaned forward, curiosity piqued, "Do y'all know where she lives? I'd like to ride by and see if that truck is there."

Clover nodded, "She lives in Ashland near the college. Her house is on the corner of College Street and Fourth. It's a neat Tudor-style brick house."

Billy's eyes lit up with recognition, "I know exactly the house you're talking about. Mom and Dad took us trick or treating over there every year when we were kids. She always had homemade popcorn balls."

Clover confirmed, "That's exactly right. As far as I know, she still makes them every year."

Brooks stood up, clapping his hands together. "Come on, boys, let's ride over there and take a look." Without hesitation, Joe, Jake, Brooks, Billy, and Chuck got in Clover's Lincoln Navigator and rode over. Bobby declined to go as he had to prepare the grill for the steaks and potatoes. He said, "I'll let y'all play detective, but get your asses back here quick."

The 15-minute ride to Ashland passed quickly, tension thick in the air as they all silently exchanged glances. Soon enough, they were cruising down College Street, the familiar route feeling different under the weight of the situation. Joe drove slowly and stopped at the corner of College and Fourth. They each looked at the Collier home and saw a beat-up, blue Chevy Colorado in the drive.

Jake leaned forward in his seat, squinting, "Well, I'll be damned. That's it, ain't it, Billy?"

Billy confirmed as Joe turned right on Fourth Avenue. As they passed, they saw a young man appear behind the house and walk towards the truck.

Billy's eyes narrowed, "That's him!" he said, his voice sharp.

Brooks said, "Damn, that fucker does look like a meth head." Saying to no one in particular, Brooks said, "Call the damn sheriff!" Chuck said, "On it, Brookie." Chuck had Buck's phone ringing as soon as his son, Billy, confirmed the truck. The sheriff thanked Chuck for the tip and said someone would be right over, but they needed to steer clear.

Buck called Antonio "Tony" Kendall, Chief of Police for Ashland PD, since it was his jurisdiction. Tony, Brooks, and Chuck attended high school, played football together, and remained in touch. There was a layer of trust built through shared history.

Brooks told his nephew to turn left into a parking lot at the college's visitor center. Joe backed the Lincoln into a space discreetly out of sight but close enough to see the events soon to occur and switched off the engine. Within ten minutes, an unmarked Ford Explorer pulled into Ellen Collier's driveway.

Brooks nudged Joe, his voice low, "That's Tony." They watched the scene and soon noticed the young man bolting across Fourth Street, running to the parking lot towards their parked SUV. When the fleeing suspect got within 20-30 feet of the Lincoln, Joe opened the door, jumped out, and, within a few seconds, had him on the ground. The man struggled for a moment before realizing he wasn't going anywhere.

Tony ran up, cuffed the man, and told Joe, "Damn boy, don't kill him before I can question him!"

Tony recognized Brooks and smirked, "You on a stakeout, Brookie? This your boy here apprehending suspects?"

Brooks grinned, "Naw, Tony, he belongs to Bobby."

Tony chuckled, shaking his head. It was clear their old camaraderie hadn't faded. He then grew serious again, nodding toward Brooks. "Buck filled me in on your tip about the Collier house. Good work."

After searching the suspect for weapons and taking his wallet, Tony identified him as Dakota Lee Kelly. The Chief also found a quarter ounce of meth and promptly placed him in the back of the Explorer. Sheriff McWaters arrived and quickly got up to speed. Even though this wasn't officially the sheriff's jurisdiction, the local police department deferred all serious crimes to the county for investigation.

Mrs. Collier and a young lady appeared from the house during the commotion. Buck and Tony greeted Ellen Collier and asked the young lady her name, and she replied, "My name is Ginny, and that's my fiancé, Dakota." her voice sharp with defensiveness. Why y'all arresting him? We ain't done nothing wrong?"

Buck's eyes narrowed as he responded firmly, "Well, what you've done has yet to be determined, but the Chief of Police has found over a quarter ounce of meth on your man out there, so he's going to jail. Now I suggest you get ready to answer some questions, young lady. Despite my respect for Mrs. Collier, I've got no choice but to request a search warrant for these premises, and if you've got something to hide, you best be coming clean now." Ginny shot a glance at Ellen Collier, who was wringing her hands and shaking her head.

Mrs. Collier said, "Ginny, you talk to the sheriff, or you can pack your bags and leave."

Ginny looked at the sheriff, and he asked, "Were you out by Lake Early this weekend?"

The girl looked down and said, her voice wavering, "I don't remember being out there." The sheriff pointed at the Chevy and said, "Well, either you were or weren't. Witnesses saw that truck and the two of you parked along a public road nearby. I'm gonna tell you right now, young lady. It would do you well to start remembering and give me some straight answers. I've got one dead body and one missing elderly lady. Now we've already got your boyfriend on meth possession, and he's headed to jail, and if we find anything here, you can join him."

Ginny smartly replied, "Well, I'll just get my shit and go. I don't have to listen to this!" Buck's expression grew angrier. His voice rose, dripping with authority, "Girl, you're gonna sit your ass down, and you're not going anywhere until the search is complete."

He turned to Ellen Collier and said, "Mrs. Ellen, I'm sorry about this. I understand she is your granddaughter."

Ellen sighed deeply, shaking her head, "Oh no, Buck, she's my great niece. My sister phoned me a couple of weeks ago asking if it would be okay if they spent a couple of days on their way to a new job in Florida. I haven't seen her in over ten years, so I agreed, but I wish I hadn't."

After Kelly was arrested, the Campbell and Langdon men returned to the Lodge and shared the events.

Jake was the first to speak up, grinning from ear to ear, "Papa, Joe clotheslined that skinny bastard, and he went down flat!"

Joe, rubbing his sore arm, winced a little, "My damn arm hurts too. Daddy, I'm gonna need the week off."

Bobby waved off his son and replied, "Leave request denied. Injuries incurred from Hulk Hogan wrestling moves are not entitled to sick leave."

The crowd broke into laughter, and Clover chuckled along, shaking her head. "Joe, you should have stayed in the car and let the police handle it. What if he'd had a gun?"

Joe shrugged, still defiant, "I could tell he didn't have anything in his hands, and I had mine on me if he went for something."

Brooks offered, "Shit, that ugly bastard didn't have time to blink, much less pull a gun from his pants. By the time he knew what was happening, Joe had his ass on the ground!"

Rooster jumped in, teasing, "Joey, say, you didn't make that boy piss himself, did ya?"

Joe smirked, "Yeah, and probably shit himself too!"

Jake snorted, adding, "Uncle Remus, I pissed myself a little bit just from watching!"

They all laughed, glad to have some lightheartedness after the day's events. But the mood shifted when John raised a question, his voice more serious, "Did y'all see the girl?"

Brooks, nodding his head, replied, "From a distance, and Jake ain't lying - 100% chicken-head white trash."

Clover added, frowning slightly, "I just can't see Ellen letting them stay for five minutes, much less overnight. I'll bet she's fit to be tied, the poor thing."

Once the search warrant arrived, four more ounces of meth were found in the couple's possessions. The warrant also included the search of the Chevy Colorado, and within minutes, a Taurus 9mm handgun and a Ryobi reciprocating saw with what appeared to be dried blood on the blade were found. The discoveries added a grim layer to the couple's charges. They were arrested, Mirandized, taken to the Sheriff's Office and placed in separate rooms for questioning.

Marie Chamblis, a 30-year veteran detective, was tasked by the sheriff to question Ginny, and Todd Anderson, a ten-year detective, interviewed her fiancé, Dakota Kelly. Marie was an old-school investigator – stout, with an ample backside, bleached blond hair teased to the ceiling, and oversized 1985-style glasses. Her appearance might have thrown some off, but her interrogation skills were razor-sharp.

She began cordial enough but soon turned serious. "Little lady, I'm just gonna tell you right now, the two of you are in a world of trouble, and you might want to start talking."

Ginny glared at her, venom in her voice. "Fuck you, you fat cunt! I want a lawyer". Marie threw her hands up and said, "You got it, Puss, your fuckin funeral," with that she left the room, letting the weight of Ginny's decision linger.

Meanwhile, Todd Anderson had a similar result with Kelly in the other interview room, so the two were sent to holding cells. The pistol, saw, and blade were taken to Atlanta for ballistics and DNA profiling.

Later, as the family gathered to eat, John received a phone call from Buck about the same time Tony called Chuck. The room quieted, listening intently. The Chief and Sheriff said the couple was their number one suspect in the murder. Without going into details, they were informed that strong evidence collected indicated their involvement. They also informed them of the couple's refusal to comment, asking them not to share the information outside the family.

Each informed the others of their call's details, and the group sat silently for a few seconds, taking in the information. A heavy cloud of realization hung over them as they absorbed the gravity of the situation. Vic chimed in on the subject for the first time. "I'll be goddamned if those two didn't kill Dave and Bernice! This is some Helter Skelter shit, for sure! I bet they were high and just picked them out of the blue. Pure ass evil, straight from the pits of Hell!"

John nodded slowly, his voice somber, "Well, I can't imagine any other explanation. Short of a hired hit or something Mafia-related, what else could there be? But who the hell would want these two dead? They are- I mean were, some of the nicest people you'd ever meet. There was no way this was a hit, and Dave wasn't in the Mafia. I'll bet the farm on that."

# Chapter 16

The following Thursday after the murders, the Sullivan County Sheriff's office received results from Atlanta indicating the DNA taken from the blood on the sawblade and Dave Lewinski's body matched. In addition, the serial number on the Taurus 9mm matched a purchase made by Hunter Cantrell, a resident of Forsyth, Georgia.

The gun had been reported stolen over a week ago when Cantrell, an airline pilot, reported a break-in at the Atlanta Airport Marriott. Mr. Cantrell often parked his F150 in the Marriott's parking lot and took the airport shuttle to the terminal instead of using employee parking if he ran late. When he arrived from a three-day leg, he found the rear passenger window of his truck broken and his 9mm missing. Buck McWaters called the DA immediately with the information.

Reggie Hobbs was the first black DA in Sullivan County's history and had been in the position for less than a year. Reggie grew up in Derany, Georgia, a small community seven miles west of Ashland, the county seat. He worked for the Fulton County DA's office in Atlanta for several years and decided to run for office in his home county.

Buck McWaters had followed Reggie's progress for a while since his mother worked for the Sullivan County Sheriff's office for 26 years. Beverly Hobbs started in the response center, taking 911 calls, and now runs the Sullivan County Emergency Management Department. Reggie was tough on crime, but most of all, he had the respect of the community, both black and white.

Reggie arrived at the sheriff's office on Friday morning and met with Buck and the public defender, Karen McElroy, a 45-year-old no-nonsense lawyer with very little tolerance for BS. Reggie told Karen, "Karen, with the evidence in front of us, it's just a matter of getting the facts. Now, I assume Kelly did the killing, but who knows? I'll not even speak of a deal until I know the location of Bernice Lewinski- or her body and Mr. Lewinski's head. I will give you an hour with your clients, and I hope you can talk some sense into them. If not, I'm putting this on a fast track with the death penalty for both of them, and I'll damn sure get it after what they did." Karen nodded in agreement and left to speak with her clients.

Karen sat in an interview room as her client, Ginny Knowles, was led in and seated across from her lawyer, still in cuffs, slumped into the chair. Ginny looked at Karen with a tilted head and an expression of inconvenience.

Karen, unamused, broke the silence first, "Oh, I'm sorry, young lady. Am I holding you up from something more enticing?"

Ginny's eyes narrowed, "Well, I just don't know why the fuck I'm in here in the first place. None of that shit was mine."

Karen leaned in, her voice low but firm, "Ginny, we are way beyond that. An ounce of meth was found in your suitcase, so you're in jail for a while. Honey, and let me tell you, that drug charge isn't shit compared to what they have on you two." Karen then began to list all the evidence against the two: The stolen gun, the sighting on Andrews Road, their prints inside the Lewinski Home, and the saw and blade. Definitely enough to get a conviction from any jury.

She said, "Ginny, just by association, you are going to jail for the rest of your life and may even get the death penalty if you don't start talking."

Ginny's head dropped, and Karen saw tears welling up when she lifted it back up. Karen said softly, "Ginny, we don't have much time. The only reason the DA is here and may offer you a deal is based on whether or not you share the location of Bernice Lewinski-or her body and Dave Lewinski's head."

Ginny hastily wiped away her tears, her gaze darting left before returning to meet Karen's stare.

"I told Dakota not to follow that lady home," Ginny continued, "We got behind the lady in the Mercedes while riding on a country road. Dakota said she was probably rich and we should follow her home and rob her. He followed her and saw her turn into their driveway. We rode on by and parked along the road."

"Is this when the two of you had sex?" Karen probed, maintaining her calm demeanor.

Ginny nodded and said, "I saw this truck coming and told Dakota, but he said, 'Just let 'em watch.'" Ginny looked away, shaking her head and paused for a moment before continuing. "We was so fuckin' high. They rode by, and they was real cute, especially that dark-skinned one. Well, we finished and shared a joint while lying in the pickup bed, and I told him we should get back to Ellen's. He said, 'Hell naw, I'm going to that house and get me some cash.'"

"And that's when everything spiraled out of control, isn't it?" Karen prompted, trying to keep Ginny focused.

Ginny swallowed hard, a flicker of shame crossing her face, "I begged him to just go back home, but he wouldn't. He pulled into their driveway and turned the lights off. He parked, grabbed that pistol he stole, and told me to wait in the truck. I sat there for maybe 10 minutes when I heard a gunshot. I moved over to the driver's seat and was about to leave when Dakota texted me, saying he was okay. I texted back, asking what happened, but he didn't reply. I cut the truck off and just waited. Next thing I know, there's another gunshot! This time, he told me to drive up to the house.

When I got there, the lady was lying in the yard face down. Dakota didn't say anything. He just got that saw out of the toolbox, went into the garage, and closed the door. He came out in a few minutes with a trash bag. I helped put the lady in the back of the truck, and we left."

Karen said, "When did you go into the house? Your prints were found in the front foyer."

Ginny hesitated before responding, "Oh yeah, I did go in there to follow him back in, but he stopped me and told me to wait."

Karen leaned forward and asked, "Ginny, what did you do with their remains?"

Ginny replied, "We drove onto a dirt road not far from there. We went about a mile, and he pulled off where some power lines crossed. He backed close to the woods and left them there."

Karen said, "Ginny, anything you say to me is confidential, and I can't disclose any of this information with the sheriff or DA without your permission, but if you don't share it, you will be tried for murder and likely convicted. If you cooperate, which means you will have to testify in court against Dakota, I believe I can get you a much lighter sentence."

Ginny leaned back in her chair and looked at the ceiling, her heart beating against her skin rapidly, "I'll say whatever I need to get out of this." Karen thanked her for the information, excused herself, and left the room.

Karen met Buck and Reggie in the hall. She informed them both of what they expected- Bernice Lewinski was deceased. She said her client had agreed to speak with the sheriff. Buck called for a tape recorder and motioned for Karen and Reggie to join him. The three crowded in the small room, and Ginny gave the same account she did earlier and agreed to sign a confession. The three left the room and entered the hall when Karen said, "Reggie, that girl in there is not guilty of murder. She's made some bad choices, but she's only 19 years old."

Nodding, Reggie replied, "Not that I need her to convict this guy, but if her story checks out, I'll agree to accessory after the fact. She does no less than ten years."

Karen asked, "Ten years, that's the best you can do?"

Reggie's expression hardened, "You damn right, and that's if she doesn't have priors. She showed her ass to the officers here when they first brought them in. She would have never told a soul if that dumbass boyfriend of hers was a better criminal."

Karen's frustration boiled over, "Fine! These two haven't given me much to work with. I'm going to speak with the dumbass boyfriend. Do you know if anyone has told him of the evidence against him?"

Reggie sighed, running a hand through his hair. "Well, secrets are hard to keep in these walls, so I'm sure he's been told, probably by another inmate."

With that Karen steeled herself and left for the following interview, determined to get to the truth.

A cuffed Dakota Kelly sat in the interview room, the cold metal of the handcuffs clinking against the table as he slumped into a chair. Karen soon entered.

"Mr. Kelly, I'm your court-appointed attorney, Karen McElroy. I understand you've been uncooperative with the police. While it is your right to remain silent, I suggest you speak with me if you want to live long enough to see gray hair." She shared the evidence with him and the gist of the conversation with Ginny Knowles.

"Mr. Kelly, Ginny has agreed to testify against you in court to receive a reduced sentence for herself." She stated, watching his reaction.

Kelly's eyes widened, anger and disbelief washing over him, "Why the hell would Ginny even be arrested? She didn't do anything! None of the dope was hers." His voice rose in indignation, but Karen locked his stare, slowly shook her head, and said, "Dakota, drugs were found in her belongings in a shared room, and she assisted in the removal of a murder victim. She's an accessory to murder and could still be tried as an accomplice if your story doesn't coincide with hers. The police are searching for the

Lewinski's remains as we speak, but I'm not here to talk about Ginny. That ship has sailed. My only job now is to keep you off death row, and that isn't going to be easy."

She leaned in closer, her voice dropping to a serious whisper, "The DA is after blood, and he's not discussing a plea for you, regardless of whether you confess. He plans to speak with Lewinski's three adult children later today, and if they choose to seek the death penalty, we are going to trial." Karen paused, allowing the weight of her words to settle over him like a heavy fog. She continued, "You are charged with killing an innocent and defenseless elderly couple while high on meth. Your actions are a textbook example of felony murder, which will carry a minimum of life in jail, but in this case, as I said, more likely the death penalty."

Kelly laid his head on the table, the reality of his situation crashing down on him as he began to sob uncontrollably. He looked up, eyes red and bloodshot, tears mingling with snot as he wiped his nose on his sleeve. When he finally composed himself, he asked, "Can I just talk with the sheriff and get this over with? I don't want to tell it more than once. I don't even care what they do with me; I just want Ginny protected." He pleaded, his voice cracking under the weight of his remorse.

Karen replied softly, "That's probably a good idea, Dakota." She left the room and returned a few minutes later with Buck and Reggie.

Kelly shared the details of the murder with the sheriff and DA. He said the garage door was open upon approaching the home. He entered the open garage and surprised Dave Lewinski, who saw the drawn pistol. Dave was holding a rake and took a swing at the intruder. According to Kelly, he fired the gun without even aiming and shot Dave in the forehead. The noise startled Bernice, who came running from the home. When she appeared, the intruder shot her in the chest while she stood in the open doorway connecting the garage and kitchen. Kelly said he removed the head to take the bullet evidence, doubting he could carry Dave's 270lb body. Buck and Reggie both looked at the murderer with contempt but sat in silence as they listened.

When the interview ended, Buck said, "What bullet evidence, Mr. Kelly? The gun wasn't registered to you."

Kelly lowered his head and replied, "I listened to a Podcast a while back about a murder on a lake somewhere in Georgia, and I thought I'd make it look like that so y'all would think it was related." A chill went down Buck's spine because he was aware of the murder and the ghastly similarities. It came up in the early hours of the investigation. Buck said he would have the confession transcribed, but he also wanted Kelly to write a signed confession listing each detail. Reggie told Kelly he would not discuss a plea to life without the possibility of parole until he spoke with the Lewinski family.

Buck and Reggie left immediately for the scene where the bodies had been discovered, just as Ginny described. In minutes, Buck and Reggie were pulling up.

Carl Stevens, the Sullivan County Coroner, greeted the men and said, "Well fellas, it's just as the girl described. One deceased Bernice Lewinski from a single gunshot wound to the chest and one severed head of David Lewinski with a single gunshot to the forehead."

The men walked to the morbid scene where the remains had been covered. Buck looked at both Reggie and Carl and said, "I'd like to get the remains released to their children as soon as possible. Carl, how much time are you going to need?"

Carl replied, "I've taken all the pictures we need. I can't imagine we'd need an autopsy here, so I'll have everything ready by tomorrow noon."

Buck nodded and looked at Reggie who replied "I don't see any reason for holding the remains based on what we have." Buck agreed and called for one of his deputies. He instructed the Deputy to get Father O'Neal on the phone. The deputy soon handed Buck the phone. Buck relayed the information to the priest including the confessions, and asked if he wanted to join him when he visited the family for the death notification. Father O'Neal informed him the Lewinski's children and grandchildren were expected at St. Matthews within the hour to take communion. He then asked if he could inform the family and when the remains would be released.

Buck replied, "Absolutely Father you are more than welcome to, and we expect to release the remains tomorrow afternoon. When you speak with them, please tell them that the DA and I will stop by to see them later this evening at the Campbell's and give more details and answer any questions. I heard they were staying at John's place on the lake." The priest affirms the information and agreed to tell them they would stop by.

Later that evening after the scene was processed and bodies removed, Buck and Reggie rode together to the Campbell's lake lodge. John and Clover reached out to Father O'Neal to offer the home to the family, as their parent's house would not be available until released by law enforcement. The men arrived and walked up the stairs to the front door. As Buck approached the door, he saw John and Clover in the kitchen. John noticed the two and came to the door. Buck introduced Reggie to the Campbells and said, "John, I assume the family is still at the church." John replied, "Yeah, they've been gone for over an hour so I expect them back soon.

Clover spoke up. "God bless that family. I tell you, fellas, they are absolutely pitiful." Buck shared the developments and confessions.

John shook his head and looked at his sister. "Damn Clover, if it ain't just like Vic said." Buck looked on, confused, and John explained Vic's earlier prediction. Reggie replied this time, "Pretty much what happened."

Clover shook her head and said, "Well, this is just the worst thing I can ever recall happening in these parts, and I'll never forget it." She continued, "Gentlemen, John and I were just cleaning up a bit, and I'm warming up some food Dottie, Julie, and I made for the family. Some ladies from their church should be here any moment with more. As soon as they come, we plan to leave to give them some privacy. They've been gone over an hour, so I expect them back at any minute."

Soon, two cars appeared with Dave and Bernice's children and grandchildren. The weather was mild, so John, Clover, Buck, and Reggie moved to the patio near the outdoor kitchen. John and Clover introduced the sheriff and DA and left.

Buck gestured for the family to take a seat, and they settled onto the patio furniture, the weight of their grief palpable in the air. Buck and Reggie offered their heartfelt condolences, their expressions somber yet compassionate. Buck informed the family of the confessions, carefully omitting the traumatic details that would only deepen their pain.

Reggie took a deep breath before speaking, "Kelly has confessed, and we can do one of two things. We can go to trial, where he will be convicted, and I will attempt to secure a death penalty, or we can plead this out to life in prison without the possibility of parole. This is 100% your decision, and I'll do whatever you wish. You don't have to give me an answer now. I expect you will want to discuss this among yourselves." The two men stood to leave when Lewinski's daughter Elaine stood and walked up to them and gave each a warm embrace. Tearing up, she said, "My family and I can't thank you enough for working so hard to find our parent's killer so soon."

Buck nodded, "Well, ma'am, I appreciate that, but honestly, we wouldn't be here if it weren't for four young men, one of them Jake Campbell. They were staying here the night of the murder and saw the two up the road. They identified the vehicle along with Kelly and Knowles. Furthermore, Knowles' Aunt visited the Campbell Vet Hospital, where she told Dottie that her niece from Kentucky was visiting. In all my years of law enforcement, I've never seen a case move this quickly. It was only by chance, and I thank God for the small blessings in a world of hurt."

Elaine responded, wiping her tears, "John and Clover told us the boys saw them. We plan to ask them to serve as pallbearers for the funeral along with our sons." Buck had kept a very professional demeanor during visit. Professional, but compassionate. However, as he listened to Elaine, his heart ached for the pain she and her family suddenly found themselves in. A large lump grew in Buck's throat and his eyes grew misty. He hugged Elaine tightly and said "I know those boys and their families, and they would consider than an honor."

The family told Buck and Reggie they would be in touch soon, and the two men left. Once they were seated in Buck's Yukon, the atmosphere shifted slightly. Buck turned and asked Reggie, "Are you hurrying to get home?"

Reggie glanced at him, curious, "No, what's up?"

Buck smiled, "I need to make one more stop."

# Chapter 17

**W**hen John and Clover left the Lewinski's, they drove to the Pump House to join the rest of the family. These gatherings were more than routine; they were a tether to the past, a reminder of their shared history and legacy. Each moment spent together strengthened the bonds that had sustained the Campbells through decades of triumph and trial. Upon arrival, they found the entire Campbell Clan, including Rooster and Sweet. Darkness had fallen for an hour, and Rooster had a nice fire going out back. The glow from the flames flickered over their faces, casting long shadows that felt as timeless as the family's legacy.

John joined Rooster, Bobby, Alex, Joe, and Andy by the fire. Each had his own quiet struggles and dreams hidden beneath their familiar faces. John's thoughts lingered on Madie, while Alex's mind was divided between family loyalty and the strain of balancing work with marriage. Clover went inside, where Dottie, Julie, Jenna, and Jake were looking through a box of old photos. Brooks and Sweet were hovering over two crock pots.

Clover inhaled deeply as the rich, savory scent of collards and beans filled the air, warming her from the inside out. She closed her eyes for a brief second, savoring the aroma, a comfort that reminded her of home and family.

"Smells good, Sweet." Clover said, smiling as she opened her eyes, "You cooking collards?"

Sweet, standing proudly by the stove, gave a nod of satisfaction. "Yep. Collards in one pot with some neckbones and beans in the other." She replied, stirring each pot gently as the steam rose around her, enveloping her in a cloud of home-cooked goodness. Brooks, hovering nearby with a spoon in hand, chimed in with a chuckle, "I've been sampling for over an hour. It's mighty fine."

Clover's stomach growled at the thought, and she laughed, patting it. "Good," she said, flashing Sweet a grateful smile. "John and I haven't eaten since breakfast."

Sweet chuckled, shaking her head. "Well, it's about time, then. Go ahead, make yourself a plate."

Another set of headlights appeared not long after John and Clover arrived, casting beams across the yard. Jake, lounging near the window, perked up, looked out the window and announced, "It's the sheriff. Better hide your weed, Dad."

Brooks chuckled, giving Jake a playful shove on the shoulder, "Hide your beer, you underage little shit." He shot back, his eyes twinkling with mock disapproval.

Buck and Reggie walked to the rear of the Pump House and joined the men by the fire, shadows dancing across their faces in the firelight. Buck tipped his hat in greeting, "I hope you folks don't mind us stopping by." He said, his voice warm and easy.

John stood, spreading his arms in a welcoming gesture, "Well, usually, I wouldn't appreciate a law dog stopping by unannounced, but you're welcome anytime, Buck, you know that."

Buck grinned back, tipping his hat a little lower as a silent thank you. He reached out, and one by one, the men clasped hands, giving firm, hearty handshakes that carried more than just introductions.

Bobby raised a brow, "You fellas want a beer?"

Buck said, "I'll take one. Reggie?"

Reggie smiled, his eyes lighting up, "Sure, I haven't had a Schneider in a while."

Bobby asked Joe, "Son, how bout getting these fellas some refreshments and bringing some extras." Joe went inside and quickly returned with a six-pack. Small talk ensued, and Buck asked, "Where's Brooks?"

Bobby smiled, jerking his head toward the house, "If you want to know where he is, just look for the womenfolk, and you'll find him."

Joe laughed, shaking his head, "Jake is just like him."

Buck raised an eyebrow and asked, "That's his boy, right?"

Bobby nodded.

Taking a moment for his tone to sober, Reggie said, "I'd like to thank him, your aunt, and your sister for all their help. Who were the other boys with Jake?"

Andy replied, "My younger brother Billy and two of their friends, Gage Turner and Tyler Wainright." Jake appeared on the back porch, taking a couple of lazy strides down the steps with his hands in his pockets as if on cue.

Brooks soon followed and joined the men around the fire.

Reggie turned to Jake, meeting his eyes with a respectful nod, "Jake, we would like to thank you for your tip regarding the Lewinski murders. We would have likely not known who did this if you boys hadn't seen those two."

Jake's usual grin softened, replaced by something quieter, almost humble, "Y'all are more than welcome." He said, his gaze dropping briefly to the ground. "I guess we were meant to be there. The thing is, we almost didn't go to the store. We caught two nice flatheads on some limb hooks and were planning to fry them up, but it was getting late, so we decided to make a quick run to the store to get some burgers." He paused, looking up thoughtfully. "We saw them on the way back. Had they already murdered the Lewinski's when we saw them?"

Reggie shook his head slowly, "No, we don't think so."

Buck offered his thanks as well and said, "We have a few loose ends to tie up, but you fellas sure made our jobs easier. "

Jake nodded, looking both men in the eyes, "I really appreciate it, sheriff. You too, Mr. Reggie. It means a lot."

Buck smiled and said, "You know Jake, you caught the girl's eye. She mentioned a cute little dark-skinned boy in her statement."

Jake stuck his finger in his mouth as if attempting to make himself vomit and said, "Well, sheriff, I catch a lot of ladies' eyes, but that one can go fornicate herself with a rusty iron pipe." Buck and Reggie both let out loud laughs.

Brooks said, "Yeah, fellas, my little biracial boy here pulls more tail than a blind kid at a petting zoo." Laughter erupted around the fire, hearty and unrestrained.

Joe, catching his breath, grinned and chimed in, grinning, "Biracial and bisexual, we suspect."

Jake rolled his eyes, grinning, "You wish! You're the one dating a girl named Blake. That sounds like some underlying gay repression for sure." Again, more laughter.

Although Brooks' comment was largely exaggerated, Jake is popular with the ladies. With wavy, jet-black hair that shimmered blue in the sunlight, he was the only one among the Campbells to inherit such striking features. Half Filipino, his hazel-green eyes were a magnet for attention—a fact his cousins never let him forget. At 5'-8", he was shorter than the other men in the family, but he didn't seem to mind that- or still being called "Baby Jake" occasionally.

Just then, the back door creaked open, and Clover appeared on the back porch and commanded the men to come in and eat. "Get y'all's asses in here and eat. Buck and Reggie, you too. I'm not taking no for an answer."

Reggie replied, "Yes, ma'am," and the group went inside.

The ladies had already helped themselves, so the men formed a line at the two crock pots.

John said, "Ladies, you all know Buck, and if you haven't already met, this is the Sullivan County DA, Reggie Hobbs." The ladies exchanged nods and friendly smiles, welcoming the newcomers as if they'd always been a part of the family. As they filled their plates, both men complimented Sweet on the food.

"Well, thank you, gentlemen," Sweet replied, giving a modest nod as she wiped her hands on a dish towel. "Brookie helped me, and he made the cornbread."

Buck raised an eyebrow in surprise, looking at Brooks with a grin, "Is that a fact? Brooks, I didn't know you could cook. I figured a confirmed bachelor like yourself would eat out of a can."

Brooks said, "Aww, hell naw- I love to cook. Bobby, too, and so does Dad."

Buck said, "Well, I don't know bout the rest of your cooking and don't tell my wife, but this is the best cornbread I've ever had."

Reggie agreed, savoring each bite, "Mrs. Hubert, I can't tell you the last time I had neckbones. My mother and wife have both gotten the idea that pork is extremely unhealthy and barely cook it anymore."

Brooks said, "Sorry to hear that, Reggie. You know I produce a lot of beef, but if I had to choose between only one for the rest of my life, the hog would have it all day long."

Both crockpots were scraped clean when Reggie and Buck left the Pump House. Rooster and Sweet soon walked home, and the Campbells sat around the wood stove. The fire crackled peacefully, and John said, "Boys, play us something before we leave."

Bobby and Brooks keep a couple of guitars at the Pump House for such occasions. Bobby said, "Daddy, do you have Paw Paw's fiddle with ya?"

John replied, "No, I'll join in next time."

With the guitars tuned, Brooks looked at his brother and said, "How about an old tune, Bobby, "The Parting Glass." "

Bobby said, "That one's a workout, but I'll give it my best."

The old Scotch-Irish folk song was Asa Campbell's favorite, a melody that echoed through the Campbell home for as long as anyone could remember. It had been played at his funeral, filling the gravesite with memories of his life – a life marked by grit and love. Before they began, Brooks held his guitar close, looking around the circle of family gathered near the wood stove. His voice softened as he said, "This is for Dave and Bernice."

Bobby began the instrumental intro flawlessly while Brooks played accompaniment and sang. The song is a popular tune played at funerals in the old country and is a tribute to a life well-lived and the promise of reuniting with loved ones again. After the brothers finished, a teary-eyed John Campbell rose from his chair, walked behind his boys, and kissed them both on the top of the head.

He said, "I needed that, boys. God knows I'm a blessed man, and I love you all more than life itself. I know I don't say often enough how proud I am of my children and grandchildren."

John's kids and grandkids returned the sentiment, and the group departed for their respective homes.

# Chapter 18

A large crowd was gathered at St. Matthews Catholic Church for the Lewinski double funeral, the air thick with whispered condolences and tearful embraces. The Campbells, Buck McWaters, and Reggie Hobbs all attended. After the service, the Lewinkis thanked the Campbells for the hospitality, and Clover assured them the lodge would be theirs for as long as they needed it. Elaine and her two brothers, Ben and Jason, walked up to Reggie and Buck. Her voice was low, almost as if she were holding each word carefully to avoid shattering.

"Thank you both for coming," she said, offering a faint, weary smile. She took a deep breath before turning to Reggie, her hands clenched together as she gathered her thoughts.

"We have discussed it," she continued, her gaze steady but pained. "The three of us agree on settling a plea with Kelly – as long as he stays in prison for the rest of his life. We just…. we don't want to go through a trial. And we want him to think about our parents every day."

Reggie's expression softened. He nodded, his eyes full of compassion and respect for her decision, "That's very generous of you three, and I'll follow your wishes. If it's any consolation," he paused, searching for the right words. "I will tell you Kelly has shown great regret for his actions. I've never seen a defendant more broken and remorseful. I suppose at the center of that dark heart lies a whiff of humanity."

Elaine's face flickered with a mixture of emotions – pain, relief, and perhaps the faintest glimmer of hope. She looked away for a moment, steadying herself, before meeting Reggie's eyes again. "I genuinely hope I can be able to forgive him one day," she said, her voice barely above a whisper, "because I've lived long enough to know hate and vengeance only hurt the person holding onto them."

Reggie offered her a warm embrace. She leaned into him, her eyes closing for a brief moment as if absorbing the strength he offered. When they pulled apart, he nodded, his hand lingering briefly on her shoulder. "I'll be in touch as soon as we have a sentencing date for Kelly." He promised.

After the funeral, Bobby left with Brooks, Jake, and Joe instead of heading home with Julie. The silence in the truck was thick; each brother lost in his own thoughts as they made their way to the brewery. Bobby and Brooks had plans to meet with Libby Maddox at the brewery. The family planned to travel the next day for their yearly Thanksgiving Holiday in the Bahamas, and the meeting is customary when the family leaves to ensure everything is running smoothly.

Libby greeted them with a warm smile and a firm handshake. They gathered around a small table in Libby's office, covering everything from production schedules to staff updates. Libby took careful notes, nodding as the brothers outlined the main points. "That should do it," Bobby said, giving Libby an approving nod.

After the three covered the bases, the brothers said goodbye to Libby and offered wishes for a Happy Thanksgiving. She did the same and joined them and their sons as they walked through the brewery floor, sharing their holiday wishes with the employees. They paused here and there, exchanging handshakes, pats on the back, and friendly smiles, their words of gratitude and cheer carrying over the soft hum of machinery.

The Campbells left the brewery and drove to the farm office to meet with Jamey Jones. Jamey is the 56-year-old farm manager who has worked for Campbell Farms since high school. Brooks calls him Mother Fucker Jones after Jamie Foxx's character in the movie, "Horrible Bosses," since he uses the term so often.

Jamie and his wife Cindy, with their 15-year-old daughter Emily, live on the Campbell farm in a home provided for them. The two found Jamey in the shop watching Luke Butler, the farm's part-time mechanic, changing a wiring harness on the farm's 1969 John Deere 4020.

With the summer crops harvested and the barley planted, there was free time to do extra chores. Jamey looked up over his readers at the Campbells, took a drag off his Marlboro Light, and said, "Y'all ain't gonna believe what that old harness looks like. I don't see how that muthafucka was working at all." He grinned, tapping ash from his cigarette into an empty beer can. With a grunt, he reached into a 55-gallon barrel used for trash, grabbed the harness, and showed the others.

He said, "Just look at this muthafucka would you?"

Brooks chuckled, crossing his arms as he inspected the harness. "Well, hell, you knew it was gone. Nothing electrical was working. We had to run a bypass wire to the lights a few years back."

Bobby rubbed the fender of the old tractor, a nostalgic smile crossing his face. "This was the first tractor I learned to operate." He said, patting the machine as if it were an old friend. "I bet I've put ten thousand miles on this old girl."

Brooks chuckled, leaning against the side, his arms crossed as he looked over the worn but dependable machine. "It's the best damn tractor on the place. This new stuff ain't shit. Half plastic, and with the government mandated emissions restrictions, the engines burn twice the fuel with half the horsepower."

Luke finished the install and said, "Brooks, I can delete that emissions program and make them just like this one here."

Brooks' eyes lit up, "Hell yeah, let's do it!" he paused, then laughed. "Wait a minute, let's ask my brother." He turned to Bobby, "Bobby, will we get in trouble if the government finds out we cut the emissions shit off our tractors?"

Bobby smirked, rolled his eyes and in the spirit of Asa said, "Hell yeah, I can see it now, 'Schneider Brewery and Schneider Farms are anti-environment!' Those woke-ass sons-a-bitches will be on us like flies on shit," he shrugged, his tone shifting to a devil-may-care drawl. "But fuck 'em. Do whatever y'all want." Brooks nodded and said "Typical government horse shit- mandate emissions restrictions on agriculture, construction equipment, and pickup trucks, but just ignore the goddamn airlines and railroads. I tell you what you do, Google a map of all the air traffic over the US right now. You won't fuckin' believe it. Now compare that to fuckin' tractors. That's how stupid your government is."

Jamey laughed, nodding his head as he flicked ash from his cigarette, "Now Brookie, you better be careful, they'll be down here measuring your cows for farts."

Brooks said, "I wouldn't doubt it. Good luck is all I can tell 'em. I've been around cows my whole life, and I'll be damned if you ever hear a cow fart. They'll piss and shit ten times an hour but never fart. At least ours never have, but Luke, the big brother, says it's okay, so hell yeah- make 'em sound like a John Deere is supposed to instead of a Briggs and Stratton."

With a chuckle, Brooks changed the subject, glancing at Jamey with a quick nod, "Jamey, you remember we're leaving tomorrow for Thanksgiving? Have any of those last heifers calved since yesterday?"

Jamey exhaled a puff of smoke, scratching his chin, "Not since this morning, but one is close. I was just about to head over there."

Brooks waved a hand, dismissing the idea. "Naw, that's okay. I'll check them after I go home and get changed. Is there anything other than those heifers I've forgotten about?"

Jamey answered, "Naw, we good, y'all have fun, and have a Happy Thanksgiving."

The Campbells returned the same and got in Brooks' F-250 to leave.

As they pulled into Bobby's driveway, Brooks looked over and asked, "You wanna go with me to check those heifers, or do you have to pack your bags?"

Bobby said, "Boy, you know damn well my wife packs my bags. Hell, what bags anyway? I keep a couple sets of drawers, shorts, and a few shirts down there." He slid out of the truck, "Yeah, I'll go with ya. I'll come over as soon as I get changed."

Joe, hopping out from the back seat, asked, "Y'all gonna need me?"

Brooks smirked, giving him a playful nudge, "Naw, I know you need to go hang out with your boyfriend- I mean girlfriend, Blake. Bobby and I can handle it."

Joe laughed it off and asked Jake, "Are you going with us this year or gonna be with your mom?"

Jake replied, "Mama is going with us this year."

Joe looked surprised and said, "Wow, that's great news! Amy is cool as shit!" Jake said, "Well, she's gonna be watching my ass down there a lot closer than Dad does, so I don't know if I like it or not."

Joe laughed and said, "You'll be okay. Love ya, Baby Jake", and blew him a kiss. Brooks and Jake headed home.

Every few years, Brooks will breed 20-30 heifers selected from calves born on the farm to replace the mature cows as they age out. When the heifers near the end of the pregnancy, they are moved from the rest of the herd to a pasture near the livestock working facilities in case of emergencies. That year, all but four had calved. First-calf heifers, as they are called, are at greater risk for complications during birth. It's not an every-year occurrence, but a calf must be pulled every so often.

When Brooks and Jake arrived home, they went inside, each with the faint sense of winding down for the day. In the small kitchen, Jake glanced over at his dad. "You need me for anything, Dad?"

Brooks said jokingly, "No, we got it. I know you got hoes to see before we leave,"

Jake snorted, rolling his eyes, "Nah. I'm going over to Rooster and Sweet's. Grady and Melody are down, and I wanna hang out with Noah."

Noah is Rooster and Sweet's 16-year-old grandson visiting from Atlanta. Brooks replied, "Tell them we'll head over after we check these heifers."

Brooks quickly changed and was outside when Bobby arrived. Brooks had the calf puller, secured it on the bed of his Polaris Ranger, and said, "I'm taking this just in case." Bobby said, "I hope not. You got beer in the cooler?"

Brooks said, "Are you fuckin' kidding me? Have you ever seen that thing empty?" Calf pullers or calving jacks are simple yet strong devices that assist in calving during a difficult birth by attaching to the calf's legs and applying slow and gentle traction to expel the calf from the womb.

They load up in the Polaris with three dogs, Brooks' border collie, Pearl, his Scottie, Hank, and Bobby's Pointer, John Henry. Pearl and John Henry were in the bed of the Polaris while Hank sat stately between the two brothers, ears alert as if on bodyguard duty. After reaching the pasture gate, Bobby hopped out and opened the gate, and Brooks drove through. They found three of the heifers together and one missing.

Brooks scanned the area, his gaze sharp and knowing, "Well, one is off to herself, probably calving."

They drove to a corner of the pasture where a few oaks and gum trees offer shade in summer. They found the heifer in labor with the calf's front hooves exposed a few inches. The heifer was lying down, breathing heavily and attempting a few strained pushes. Brooks hopped off the Polaris and squatted beside the heifer. He examined the calf's hooves and said, "She's been pushing for a while. Let's see if we can get her in the holding pen."

Brooks nudged the animal, but she remained in place. He felt her nose, which he found cold and dry. He said, "Dammit! You ain't gonna believe this! Looks like the girl has milk fever. Call Dottie and tell her I need some calcium."

Dottie and Jenna pulled up a few minutes later in the vet truck. Dottie stepped out, surveying the scene, "This girl needs some calcium, huh?" she said, already reaching for her gear.

Brooks nodded, his brow furrowed with concern, "Looks like it. She can't stand or push this calf out."

Dottie knelt and donned an exam glove that covered her right hand and arm. She lubricated the glove and began to examine the heifer's birth canal. She glanced at Brooks, "Her pelvis is dilated enough, and the calf is alive and in position. I guess she's just too weak to push. I'd like to try and get this calf out before I give her calcium." Brooks quickly placed the calf pullers against the heifer's hips and hooked the draw chains to the calf's exposed legs. He slowly began to work the ratchet, applying force to the chains and the calf. As he applied more pressure, the cow let out a distressful bellow. Dottie said, "Hold up, Brookie, wait till she pushes again."

Soon enough, the heifer pushed, and Brooks ratcheted down a few more clicks.

The heifer's breathing steadied, and after a moment, she strained, her whole-body tensing. Brooks responded, ratcheting down a few more clicks. His eyes narrowed as he worked, his hands steady, but his jaw clenched with concentration. Suddenly, the calf's snout appeared, and the head was soon exposed, slick and trembling.

Dottie said, "Just hold what you have and wait till she pushes again." Jenna quickly knelt beside her mother and cleaned off the calf's nostrils. The heifer pushed again, and Brooks worked the pullers several more clicks until the front shoulders appeared. The heifer caught her breath and strained again. With a few more ratchets and one last strained push from the heifer, the calf slid to the ground in a tangle of legs and hooves. Jenna quickly attended to the newborn.

"It's a boy, and he's breathing!" she called out, a proud grin breaking across her face. The heifer had laid her head flat against the ground, completely spent from the ordeal.

Dottie asked Jenna to retrieve an IV kit with a 500 ml bottle of calcium glutamate and instructed her as she placed the large bore needle in the heifer's jugular vein. Jenna connected the IV tube, and the fluid was soon flowing. Dottie next drew up a dose of medication to aid in the expulsion of the afterbirth. Within 10 minutes of the calcium being administered, the heifer was up and attending to her new baby.

Dottie said, "Jeb will be available next week while we're gone if Jamey needs him." Brooks said, "Yeah, he knows, but hopefully, this will be our only emergency." Brooks then asked his sister if she and her family were coming to the Pump House, reminding her that Rooster and Sweet's son, Grady, was home with his family.

She replied, "Yeah, I'm coming over. I'm bringing some leftover chicken salad from a baby shower we had for one of the girls at the hospital. Alex is at the airport going over the plane. He hasn't flown it since the new radio was installed, so I don't know when he will be home. You know how he is with a new airplane toy."

Brooks laughed, "Oh, I know, but it wasn't just a radio." The 1989 Cessna was due for its annual inspection in August, and Bobby and Alex decided to upgrade to all glass displays.

Bobby said, "Yeah, that new toy for your husband cost us over $150,000."

Dottie looked surprised, "Well, while you two are in a money-spending mood, I need a new ultrasound machine for the hospital."

Bobby laughed, "I'm spent out, honey! Tell your husband to buy it. He's making more than any of us!"

After dark, the Campbells arrived at the Pump House, and Rooster, Sweet, Grady, and his wife Melody soon walked over. Brooks was the first to greet Grady, saying, "Well, hello there, tall, dark, and handsome!" He hugged Grady and Melody, kissing her on the cheek.

The rest of the family exchanged hugs and greetings, and Clover asked, "Where's Noah?"

Melody laughed, shaking her head, "Jake stopped by about an hour ago and picked him up."

Bobby snorted, crossing his arms with a smirk, "Uh-Oh, they down by the river twistin' one up."

Melody's eyes widened, her mouth dropping open in feigned shock, "Bobby Campbell, hush your mouth!" She gave Brooks a knowing look, one eyebrow raised. "Well, I can only imagine where they got it from?"

Brooks laughed and said, "I'm sure Jake would if he wasn't afraid of getting tested and losing his baseball scholarship." Brooks referred to Coastal State University in Savannah, where Jake was offered a full athletic scholarship for the following year.

Grady said, "Daddy told me about that. I know you are proud."

Brook's expression softened, and he nodded, "Thanks, and yeah, I am. I'm blessed for sure. That boy hasn't ever given me or his mother a bit of trouble. He's a better son than I was."

John chimed in, "You weren't all that bad. I didn't have to put my foot in your ass but once or twice."

Grady said, "Well, I remember one of those times. Mr. John, did you ever find all the pieces of that old '73 Chevy that this joker crashed in the ditch?"

John said, "God, no. He fucked it up for sure. Damn lucky he didn't die." John referred to an episode when a beer-drunk 16-year-old Brooks crashed the farm's old service truck in a drainage ditch. He was chasing an armadillo across the pasture and lost control. The truck flipped, rolled a couple of times, and ended upside down in the ditch. He walked over a mile to Clover's house with a broken collar bone and concussion.

Brooks said, "Dad took my license for six months after that."

John replied, "You got away easy."

"The baby always does." Bobby replied with a smirk.

Melody turned to Clover with a warm smile, "I understand you all are heading to the Bahamas tomorrow?"

Clover sighed, giving a small, tired smile, "Yes, and after the last few week's events, I sure am ready to get away."

Melody nodded her head and said, "I know, right? Grady's folks called us last week and told us about it, and then we saw it on the Atlanta news. I saw it on two local stations, and Grady heard it on WSB Radio while driving to work. We saw the interview of Jake, Chuck's son Billy, and the other boys. It sounded like they really helped the police."

Clover said, "The sheriff says if they hadn't offered the information, we may never know who killed the couple. The only fingerprints found belonged to the girl and weren't in the system."

Melody shook her head, frowning, "Well, it's just awful, but at least they got the murderer."

Clover nodded, then shifted the conversation with a smile, "Y'all came down early this year. Usually, we don't see you before we leave for the beach."

Melody said, "Yeah, Grady is slowing down and letting some of the younger docs take up the slack, and it's about time."

Clover said, "Well, I know Rooster and Sweet are thrilled. He told me the other day that he was done driving to Atlanta to see y'all." Sweet called from their back porch for her family to come home and eat.

She yelled out, "You white folks hungry?" Clover laughed and replied, "We'll eat light tonight since we will be pigging out all week. Dottie has some chicken salad, but thanks!"

The Huberts left, and the Campbells headed inside, where a nice fire roared in the stove. The mild weather enjoyed earlier in the week had turned cooler, and it felt like late November should in Georgia.

John asked, "Has anyone talked to Alex? Is our old bird ready to go tomorrow?"

Bobby nodded, "He and Joe took it up to check the new display. They should be back by now." Alex taught Joe to fly in his teens, but he's never flown a plane with a glass cockpit.

Just then, headlights appeared in the front windows, and Brooks said, "Speak of the devil, and here they are." Alex and Joe entered the front door, and Joe told his dad how nice the new cockpit was.

Bobby said, "Good, you can fly us to the beach tomorrow."

Joe looked over at Alex, "Uncle Alex, you gonna let me have the left seat tomorrow?" Alex grinned, slapping Joe on the back, "Hell yeah, I can start drinking early."

Jake, leaning against the wall, chimed in. "I'm ready for snorkeling at No Name Cay. We gotta get some lobsters on the table for Thanksgiving."

Lobster season runs from August to March in the Bahamas, and a family tradition is taking the Yellow Fin out for a day of snorkeling and lobstering.

Jenna's eyes sparkled as she raised an eyebrow at her cousins, "Me too; I'm ready to beat you boys again this year in the lobster catch."

Joe shot her a playful look, crossing his arms, "I'm all for letting the women catch and cook my dinner."

She narrowed her eyes, her hands on her hips, "Boy, you'll eat PB&J's before I cook for you!"

Joe laughed, walked up to his cousin, and gave her a big bear hug, picking her off the ground.

Clover announced, "Okay, family, let's all clean up and get some sleep. We have a busy day tomorrow."

# Chapter 19

The family traveled to the Sullivan County Airport Monday morning under a bright blue sky, the sun glinting off the wings of parked planes. The air buzzed with the faint hum of engines, mingling with the chatter of a few locals. Everyone kept personal items and clothes at the beach house, so not much luggage was needed.

Alex and Joe arrived an hour earlier to do the pre-flight checks, file a flight plan, and get the Caravan from the hanger to the ramp for passenger loading. Joe climbed out of the cockpit with a clipboard in hand and a grease smudge on his cheek, looking every bit the part of a hands-on pilot. He flashed a thumbs-up.

Julie standing by the car, holding her passport and customs form, did her usual roll call. "Does everyone have their customs declarations and passports?" She asked in that mom tone that didn't leave room for excuses. Each family member confirmed, and Julie scanned their faces anyway, just to be sure. "Good," she said, with a quick nod and the family loaded in the Cessna. Boarding the plane was second nature by now, though there was still the usual shuffle for seats.

Joe was already back in the cockpit, running through the last of the checklist with Alex. After making sure everything was in order, Joe taxied the Caravan to the runway and placed the plane in takeoff position. His jaw tightened slightly as the plane rumbled into position.

"All right," he muttered, half to Alex and half to himself. "Let's get this bird in the air,"

He radioed their position and applied full power to the plane's engine. Soon, the aircraft was airborne and headed south for the 2.5-hour trip. At 7,000 feet, Joe turned on the autopilot, leaned back in his seat and grabbed the mic with a grin. "Ladies and gentlemen, I'd like to thank you for flying with us today at Campbell Airlines. As always, if there's anything your crew can do to make your flight more comfortable, please ask our flight attendant, Jenna." He paused for the effect, his tone turning playful. "She will most likely tell you tell you to kiss her ass, but please don't hesitate." Laughter erupted in the cabin. Jenna rolled her eyes but couldn't hide her smirk.

Brooks wasn't about to let the moment pass. Leaning back in his seat with a mischievous grin, he asked Jenna, "Ma'am, I'd like to request another seat assignment. The lady next to me is making unwelcome sexual advances."

Amy rolled her eyes and said sarcastically, "Oh, I just can't help myself. It must be a combination of the cow shit on your boots and that ten-cent aftershave you wear. Jesus Brooks, why did you wear those?"

Brooks looked down at his mud-caked boots with a sheepish smile, "I put them on this morning when I checked the heifers and forgot to change back to my loafers." He admitted, rubbing the back of his neck. "No worries, though. I keep flip-flops at the beach."

Amy groaned, covering her face with her hand, but her lips twitched as if she was fighting back a smile. Jenna snorted, shaking her head.

The trip passed quickly, and Joe soon had the airport in sight. After a smooth touchdown, the plane taxied to the assigned parking area. After Joe and Alex tied down the Caravan, the group walked to the terminal, where Percy Bethell was waiting to take them to their vacation home. They quickly cleared customs, and the clan loaded up in Percy's 15-passenger van for the short trip to the beach house.

Percy owns a taxi service, has known the Campbells for several years, and keeps an eye on their place when vacant. John, Madie, and Clover met him when they first came to the Bahamas in search of real estate. The agent they were working with put them in touch with Percy, and they soon became friends with him and his wife, Belinda.

The Campbells arrived at the beach house and found Belinda preparing lunch in the kitchen, which she had stocked with groceries for the family's week-long stay. After the family got settled into their rooms for the week, they gathered on the oceanside-covered porch and sat with the Bethell's for a delicious Bahamian lunch. Belinda had prepared conch salad, johnny cakes, baked crab, and broiled lionfish with peas and rice.

Bobby looked up from a clean plate, leaning back in his chair with a satisfied grin, and told Belinda, "Miss Belinda, I've been looking forward to some of your island cooking for weeks, and you didn't disappoint."

The rest of the family offered additional praises, and Belinda returned the compliments with humble thanks.

"Who's turn is it to do the dishes? John asked, stretching back in his seat, a sly grin tugging at the corner of his mouth as if hoping he wouldn't get roped in.

Andy replied, "Jenna and I have it covered. What's everyone doing?"

Alex pushed his chair back, standing up with a stretch. "I'm going to the liquor store." He announced, slipping his hands into his pockets with a casual shrug. Belinda doesn't mind picking up a few groceries to stock the Campbell home but will not darken the doors of a liquor store as she and Percy are strict teetotalers.

Bobby stood up with a clap of his hands, "I'll go with you." He said to Alex, his eyes lighting up. "Let's stop by the marina and check the boat. Brooks, you going?"

Brooks responded, "Nah, we have plenty of beer here, and I brought some happy gummies. I'm heading to the beach with the ladies."

Joe, who had been quietly stacking his utensils, glanced over at Jake. "We're heading to the tackle shop," he said, his voice casual but purposeful. "Need to pick up some bait for surf fishing." Jake nodded, already halfway out of his chair.

The guys left for their marina. Dottie and Julie got dressed for an afternoon of sun and relaxation on the beach. Amy and Brooks headed to their room to change, and he said, "You know, Amy, we pretty much have the place to ourselves except for Daddy and Clover, and they're on the back porch having a cocktail. How about you and I make another baby?"

She looked at him with a mischievous smile and said, "Brookie, I'm done having babies, but I'm overdue, boy, that's for sure!" Brooks slowly removed his Columbia button-up and approached her, exposing his thick yet muscular frame. He looked down into her brown eyes and said, "I'm so glad you decided to come this year, and not just because of this."

He tilted his head down, brushing a soft kiss on her lips, his hands gently caressing her sides as he grasped her backside with both hands, pulling her closer to him. His fingers traced lightly along her skin, a slow, deliberate movement, as his lips pressed against hers, deepening the kiss. His hands slowly moved to the front, and he unbuttoned her blouse and unsnapped her bra, exposing her breasts where his lips soon found themselves. As his lips brushed against her skin, she let out a soft sigh, a shiver running down her spine.

She responded by pulling him closer, her hands moving with gentle urgency to unbutton his jeans. With a quick but tender movement, she slid a hand beneath his boxers, her fingers brushing against his skin, sending warmth through him. They paused, looking at each other for a moment, eyes meeting with shared longing before they fell back onto the bed. The room's shutters were open, and they felt the gentle breeze from the ocean, adding to the caressing of their bare bodies. Brooks gently slid his hands down her sides, his fingers brushing lightly over her skin as he carefully unzipped her jeans. He paused for a moment, his eyes meeting hers with a look of quiet intensity before he slowly eased the fabric down. As the jeans reached her ankles, he helped her lift each leg, removing them with a gentle tug, all while never breaking eye contact, his hands lingering on her legs for a moment longer than necessary.

As the air between them thickened with anticipation, Brooks' breath quickened, his fingers trembling slightly as they traced her curves. His heart pounded in his chest; each beat syncing with the rising desire that pulsed through him. Slowly, he leaned down, pressing his lips against hers in a deep, tender kiss, as if trying to memorize the feel of her.

"It's been too long," he whispered against her mouth, his voice rough with longing.

He could feel the heat between them building, her soft sighs, and the gentle curve of her body urging him closer. His hands moved down to her hips, his touch firm but gentle, as he eased himself into her.

The world outside seemed to fade away, leaving only the rhythmic sound of their breaths and the overwhelming connection between them.

She gasped softly, her fingers clutching at his back, and he couldn't help but respond to her every movement, the chemistry between them igniting all over again.

Their movements became more urgent, their hands gripping each other as they pulled closer as if they couldn't get enough. The heat between them intensified, their breaths growing quicker, more ragged. She arched her back, urging him deeper, and he responded with a soft groan, his fingers digging into her skin as if to hold onto the moment. Their bodies moved in sync, the rhythm becoming frantic, desperate, as they both felt the growing pressure, the undeniable pull towards the inevitable. They gasped in unison, their eyes meeting for a brief second before the world around them seemed to explode in a rush of overwhelming sensation.

The two lay in silence, catching their breath and enjoying the peaceful sounds of the ocean and birds singing. Soon, Brooks was snoring softly, and Amy showered and dressed for the beach.

On the way to the beach, Amy stopped on the back porch and sat with John and Clover. Clover said, "Honey, I'm so glad you came with us. When Brooks stopped by the office the other day to bring Hank in for an allergy shot, he told me you were coming. You could see the excitement in his eyes."

John leaned forward slightly, resting his elbows on his knees, "We sure are. Brooks loves you so much, and so do we."

Her face softened, and her eyes glistened, "I love you too, and I'm so thankful your family has been patient with our relationship. I've tried to honor my family's wishes all these years, and I know it seems ridiculous to 'normal' families." Her voice wavered slightly as she continued, "My parents are so narrow-minded, but they have mellowed some. Not long ago, I told my father that I felt as though they would rather see me unhappy than follow my heart. I also told him your family has more faith than any church member or priest I know."

Clover nodded; her gaze thoughtful. Amy's words clearly touched her, and she leaned forward slightly, her hands clasped in her lap.

"When Miss Madie passed so unexpectedly," Amy went on, her voice softening as she glanced toward the trees, "I thought Brooks would be a basket case. They were so close, but he handled her death with such grace." She paused, her expression bittersweet, "He said, 'Death is an illusion, Amy. Mama isn't here in a physical form anymore, but her spirit is alive and well, and I feel her presence with me every day, and I know I'll see her again.'"

Clover's face softened, and she tilted her head slightly, a small, knowing smile playing on her lips. "Amy," she began, her voice gentle. "I know many in our community see us Campbells as 'unchurched' and even 'ungodly,' but that's because we don't fit into their stereotype of what they believe a follower of God should be. Our parents taught John and me that we are all God's children, and John, Madie, and I have reinforced that to their children and grandchildren. I believe that God loves us and wants us to be happy!"

John grinned, leaning back in his chair with a playful twinkle in his eye, "Damn right, Ben Franklin said that's why God gave us beer because he loves us and wants us to be happy." Amy laughed softly, shaking her head, but her expression turned thoughtful as John continued. "Amy, have you heard the story of how my parents lost their two oldest children?"

She replied, "Yes, Brooks has told me, and I teared up when I first heard it."

He nodded and said, "In my mother's vision, she asked God, 'Why did you take my children?' Mother said the reply was, 'Your children are with me, and beauty comes of all things.'"

Amy slowly shook her head and said, "He didn't mention that. What a profound and beautiful promise!"

"My mother awoke with the peace of knowing my brother and sister are alive but, in another dimension, and I know that is true as surely as I know that my youngest is standing behind me." He turned slightly, his grin widening as he called out, "Thought you'd sneak up on the old man, Brookie?"

Brooks smiled, kissed his dad on the left cheek, and said, "I know I can't pull one on you, Daddy. Amy, I figured you'd be at the beach with the girls by now." She said, "I was, but I stopped by to talk to Papa and Clover." Brooks asked, "Have the guys come back yet?"

Clover said, "No, not yet. You'll have to play with the girls until the boys return."

"Fine with me," he said, shrugging. The two walked to the beach and placed their chairs next to Julie, Dottie, Jenna, and Andy. The weather was perfect, and so was the water.

Brooks said, "Andy, let's set up the fishing poles. If we don't, Bobby and Alex will scold us for lollygagging." The men headed to the house to gather the tackle, poles, and pole stands. Dottie opened a cooler beside her chair and told Amy, "We've got a gallon of pre-mixed Bahama Mamas. Would you like some refreshment?" Amy gleefully passed her Yeti tumbler to Dottie and said, "I've been visiting with Aunt Clover and Papa on the veranda. I can't tell you all enough how happy I am to be here this year. It's truly been too long!"

Julie replied, placing a warm hand on Amy's shoulder, "Darlin, we feel the same way. Joe was beaming with delight when he came home last night after Jake informed him you were coming." Amy smiled, her eyes gleaming with nostalgia. "He's always been my little buddy." Soon, the entire Campbell family was on the beach, the sound of waves crashing and seagulls calling blending into the perfect soundtrack for the afternoon. The guys had their lines cast with the terminal ends baited with live shrimp. Jake, Joe, and Andy sat up a tent for shade, and the Jimmy Buffet station played on Spotify.

The following day, after breakfast, Percy arrived to take the family to the marina for a day on the water. The Yellow Fin, named "Madie Bird," was docked and fueled up for a day on the water. Alex took the helm and ferried the group to No Name Cay. No Name Cay is often called "Piggyville" by locals due to the number of pigs inhabiting the area. While many vacationers and cruise line passengers are familiar with pigs on Exuma, the upper cays of the Bahamas are less well known for "swimming pigs." Like all cays, fresh drinking water is unavailable, so locals installed a 2000-gallon tank to supply the animals with fresh water. The trip from Treasure Island to No Name took approximately 30 minutes, and the boat was soon anchored twenty yards from the beach.

Jenna was the first to jump in, saying, "The last one in is a rotten egg!" Andy, Joe, and Jake soon followed and swam toward the beach, where three young pigs instantly spotted them. They brought table scraps of fresh vegetables, fruit, and live shrimp in mesh scalloping bags. The pigs swam out to greet them and gladly took the snacks. Jake bear-hugged the smallest of the pigs and held her up, facing the boat. He yelled to John, "Papa, I've caught our dinner already!"

John responded with a thumbs-up. Jenna thumped him on his head and said, "Put that pig down!" Jake swam off with his pig halfway, shouting, "No! I'm just kidding, though. I won't eat her, but I may take her home." He kissed the pig on the head and said, "Come on, Vivian, let's get away from the mean girl."

Jenna pressed her lips together, slightly amused by his comment, "Vivian? Jake Campbell, you truly are the only person in the world who would name a pig Vivian." Jake looked back as he escaped with his pig and stuck out his tongue tauntingly.

Once on shore, Jake laid back in the shallow surf and pulled a few shrimps from the front pocket of his swimming trunks. He said, "Here, Vivian, I always keep some on hand for such an occasion." The young spotted pig took the treat and sat beside Jake in the surf. Jake then took a shrimp and placed it halfway under his trunks. Vivian immediately pushed her snout under his trunks for the snack. By this time, Joe had waded over.

Jake said, "Vivian, what a naughty girl you are."

Joe, fighting back laughter, replied, "Boy, that pig is gonna mistake your shrimp dick for a real shrimp."

Jake shot him a deadpan look and said, "Nah, I tucked it between my legs."

Joe burst out laughing, his shoulders shaking as he leaned forward, the water rippling around him. He reached down to pull his cousin from the surf. "C'mon, crazy, let's not give this pig any more ideas."

With no more snacks offered, Vivian snorted in disappointment and scampered off, her little tail wagging as she joined the rest of her pack.

The rest of the Campbell family arrived and gathered in four feet of water with more pig delicacies. Clover turned to John, her hands on her hips and a bemused smile on her face. "I just can't imagine what Daddy would say if he saw us feeding pigs in the ocean."

Bobby said, "He'd say we have lost our minds, and he'd be right!"

John said, "Yeah, kinda like when Mama bought that charcoal grill from Sears in the early '50s. We had running water in the house for a few years, but Daddy kept and used the outhouse. He saw Mama cooking outside on the grill and said, 'It's a crazy world we live in. Folks are shittin' in the house and cookin' in the yard.'" Everyone in earshot laughed, and Brooks said, "I haven't heard that one before."

After feeding the pigs, the Campbells took the short trip to Green Turtle Cay for an afternoon of snorkeling along with lobster and conch hunting. Alex placed the Madie Bird near a coral reef where a GPS plot for anchoring was saved on the boat's navigation system. The water depth is 18-20 feet and crystal clear, allowing boaters to anchor visually without disturbing the reefs. Several species of colorful fish and even the occasional shark can be found among the reefs. Lobsters are most active in the late afternoon but can be found almost any time in or around the reefs and are collected by spearing the crustacean.

Once the Yellowfin was anchored and the three 400 HP engines shut down, a lunch of fried shrimp and conch 'po boys was enjoyed, and the group soon entered the crystal clear water. The view below was impressive, like something out of a Guy Havey painting. The vibrant colors of the reef sparkled in the water-filtered sunlight, and dozens of Bahama reef creatures swam below the boat. Blue and rainbow parrotfish were spotted, as well as coneys and various species of grouper.

The Campbell grandchildren grabbed their spears and began the lobster hunt. Andy was the first to score and surfaced with a hefty lobster and conch. However, the day's winner was Joe, with four lobsters and three conchs. Nearing sunset, Alex announced, "Anchors Up! The boat was soon marina-bound with her limit of ten lobsters and six conchs for Thanksgiving Dinner.

The next day, Wednesday, the family departed after lunch for more spearfishing. They bypassed Piggyville and took the Madie Bird beyond Green Turtle Cay to Nunjack Cay, where Alex anchored in a cove on the island's north end.

The only spearfishing device legal in the Bahamas is called a Hawaiian Sling. The device is straightforward and similar to a slingshot. It is made of a wooden tube with an elastic loop at the end. A shaft with a spearhead is passed through the hollow tube and pulled back, stretching the elastic loop.

Joe was the first to score with a hefty flounder. Next, Jenna tagged a lobster. Within two hours, the family took enough for a hearty Thanksgiving feast. As the golden hues of sunset painted the sky, casting long shadows over the water, the crew made their way back home. Bobby carried the cooler inside, grinning as he declared, "This is gonna be one hell of a Thanksgiving!"

Thanksgiving dinner at the Campbell's beach house has been a tradition for several years. While most families across the country feast on turkey, green bean casserole, stuffing, or dressing, depending on whether north or south of the Mason Dixon, the Campbells eat fresh seafood and sides from the Caribbean. After the meal and the cleanup, most of the family gathered on the oceanfront veranda.

Joe asked his family, "Y'all ready to cover Fleetwood Mac tomorrow night?"

Dottie, lounging with a glass of iced tea in hand, laughed and shook her head, "I've been practicing at the office so much during surgery that I'm sure the staff are ready to kill me!" Brooks, stretched out in a chair with a hand resting on his full stomach, groaned theatrically. "I'm good, but if you want to practice, it's gonna have to wait. My belly is too full to sing."

Joe referred to a gig the family planned to play at the Conch Bar and Grill on Friday night.

The Campbells had played the venue following Thanksgiving for the last few years. The first year was not planned. The family went to the restaurant on the Friday after Thanksgiving a few years back. The band scheduled to perform had cancelled a few hours before the event due to an untimely death in the lead singer's family. The bar had a piano and a couple of guitars, so Bobby, Dottie, and Brooks offered to fill in at the last moment. They were an immediate hit, and the Conch had requested they play each Friday following Thanksgiving.

This Conch crowd is mainly middle-aged crowd. Dottie suggested covering the "Rumours" album that year since it was such a big hit at recent wedding they played. Dottie, Brooks, and Jenna expertly cover Stevie Nicks, Christine McVie, and Lindsey Buckingham's vocals. Bobby called Jason Westbury, the Conch's proprietor, a few weeks back and pitched the idea. Jason didn't take a second to consider as he was thrilled and began promoting the event the next day. He phoned Bobby back the next week and said the reception to the event had been enormous, and he couldn't wait for Thanksgiving weekend.

The Campbells arrived at the Conch by 5:00 Friday to set up and practice a few numbers. By 6:00, the crowd began to grow, and by starting time at 7:00, standing room only when Brooks began with "Second Hand News." He also sang Buckingham's lead on "Never Going Back Again" and "Go Your Own Way." Dottie covered Nicks' on "Dreams," "Gold Dust Woman," "Silver Springs," and "I Don't Want To Know" with Brooks. Jenna sang McVie's part on "You Make Loving Fun," "Songbird," "Oh Daddy" and "Don't Stop" with Brooks. Bobby, Joe, and Jake provided the background harmony. When the set ended with Dottie, Jenna, and Brooks all singing lead on "The Chain," the atmosphere in the Conch was on fire. Everyone was on their feet when the song ended, offering a resounding ovation. Someone in the back yelled, "Me and Bobby McGee!" Brooks took a mic and said, "I tell y'all what. We'll do Bobby McGee if everyone sings along and Dad and Aunt Clover sing lead!" Brooks waved for John and Clover to join them onstage. Clover took her place at the piano, and John took Brooks' guitar. The crowd cheered and sang along as requested. When the song ended, the crowd begged for more, and John said, "Folks, I know my kids are tired, but I'll tell you what, if they can keep up, we'll do two more!"

More applause came from the crowd, and John turned to Bobby and said, "Elvis and Ray Charles." The music started, and John sang "Suspicious Minds" and ended with "Georgia On My Mind." When the last song ended, John said, "Georgia is on our minds, folks, and we'll be heading back to the Peach State tomorrow, but we want to offer our heartfelt thanks to each of you for such a warm welcome at the Conch!" Again, the crowd erupted, and when the applause diminished, several people came forward to meet the Campbells and offered praise.

After breakfast, Percy arrived to take the Campbells to the airport on Saturday morning. Joe took control of the Caravan and set a course for Ft. Pierce, FL, for customs re-entry to the States. Thirty minutes later, they were homeward bound. When they touched down again, Bobby said as they taxied to the hanger, "The Bahamas is beautiful, but damned if it ain't good to be back in Sullivan County."

John smiled slightly, "Son, the older you get, the less you want to leave. I can promise you that."

Brooks grasped Amy's hand and leaned over to give her a peck on the cheek. "I'm so glad you came this week. I love having all my family together."

She smiled and said, "I'm glad I did too, Brookie."

Julie asked, "Amy, we're decorating at the big house tomorrow if you want to come help. There'll be mimosas and cheese straws!"

John's house is often called the "Big House" by the family, and the ladies decorate for Christmas each year on the Sunday after Thanksgiving. Julie is a retired schoolteacher but has worked part-time as an interior decorator for several years. The ladies all agreed to meet at John and Clover's on Sunday morning at 10:00.

# Chapter 20

The Campbell Family has celebrated the Christmas holiday for over a hundred years in the home where John and Clover now live. Christmas was always a joyous occasion for Asa and Katie due to the twins' birthday, and the tradition continues when they join for meals, fellowship, and music.

The home is simply and tastefully decorated with vintage-inspired ideas. Pine cones, small cedar branches, and sprigs of holly are scattered throughout the rooms, adding a simple but festive vibe. You can almost hear the crackle of a fireplace, even if it's just in your imagination. On the front porch, a homemade wreath made of twigs, dried flowers, and bright red berries welcomes everyone who stops by. The tree is decorated with ornaments from old pictures taken from the farm and brewery over the 100-year history. Strings of dried orange slices and small bundles of cinnamon sticks hang alongside the ornaments, giving the air a festive aroma and making the house smell like the holidays. Around the room, vintage lanterns glow softly, casting a warm light that makes everything feel even more magical. There's a quiet magic in the air; the kind that makes you want to linger a little longer and soak it all in. As the ladies gathered on Sunday morning for the annual decorating, John played gopher for retrieving decor, tools, or items they needed from the attic.

The Sunday following Thanksgiving in Sullivan County was unusually cold for late November, the kind of chill that seemed to seep into your bones. Inside the house, however, it was lively and warm as the ladies bustled about, draping garlands and hanging ornaments.

Done with his chores for a while, John sat by the fireplace with the K-9 companions and sipped a Bloody Mary while snacking on cheese straws and reading last week's paper, its edges slightly crinkled. As John turned the page, movement caught his eye. He noticed Daisy first. The black Scottie sat alert, ears perched and tail wagging, looking towards the kitchen. Jack then rose and walked toward the kitchen with head low and tail wagging. He joined Daisy, and both dogs stood side by side and looked up as if someone was speaking to them. John watched, intrigued. A smile tugged at the corners of his mouth when he noticed how both dogs lowered their heads as though they were being petted by an unseen hand.

"Hey, Cora," John murmured gently. Both dogs turned to look at John, then back into their previous gaze at what appeared as thin air, but John knew who they saw. Since he was a boy, John and Clover had sensed their older sister's presence, but Clover was the first to display recognition when the twins were five.

Katie was in the kitchen rinsing dishes when the sound of her daughter's laughter drifted in. She first thought it to be the usual chatter of a five-year-old, but it seemed more conversational. She walked towards her daughter's bedroom and suddenly froze when she heard Clover say, "Oh Cora, thank you!" Katie waited in the hall to listen. Clover giggled, a carefree melody and said, "I like your dress too, Cora. Blue is my favorite color."

Katie felt her knees weaken. She instinctively raised her hand to her mouth as if to quelch a scream. Could this be a coincidence? Perhaps Clover made up an imaginary friend based on stories of her older sister, she thought. The thought flitted through her mind, but it did little to calm the storm of emotions welling within her. Her older daughter, Cora, had been gone for years. "Could it be possible" Katie softly whispered. Katie decided not to interrupt her daughter and returned to the kitchen. Not long after, Clover walked in for a drink of water. Katie said, "Clover, it sounds like you're having a lovely tea party today. Did anyone come to join you?

Clover casually said, "Yes, Ma'am, Cora came."

Katie steadied herself, her heart pounding, "Good, having tea with friends is always enjoyable. Where does Cora live, honey?"

Clover answered with the simplicity of a child, "She used to live in my room, but now she lives in Heaven."

Katie was visibly shaken but regained composure for her daughter's sake and said, "Baby, what did Cora wear to the party?"

Clover responded, "A pretty blue dress with white flowers and white around her neck." The description was unmissable. Katie instantly recognized the dress. Cora's favorite dress was blue with white daisies and lace around the collar. She was buried in the dress. Tears welled in Katie's eyes as memories of her late daughter flooded her mind.

Katie handed her daughter the water, and Cora skipped back to her room. Katie sat in one of the chairs around the small kitchen table. She was, understandably, shocked by Clover's revelation, but as she sat silently, a memory reoccurred. During Katie's vision, she asked the spirit, "Why did the Lord take my children?" The spirit replied, "Beauty comes of all things." Katie dropped to her knees and prayed that afternoon, thanking God for his promises and her two healthy and happy children. The promise had come full circle. Cora was gone, but her presence lingered, a reminder of love that never truly fades.

When Asa arrived home with John, Katie told her husband of the tea party. Asa listened and responded, "Katie, my life has been marked by tragedies and salvation. God knows it's only by his hand I found a loving home instead of an orphanage after losing my parents. Meeting and falling in love with you and ending up here - was that all coincidence? I don't believe so. Our Earthly existence is but a short time in the lives of our souls. I know Thomas and Cora's spirits are alive as sure as I know you are sitting in front of me, and if our sweet Cora somehow shows herself to Clover, should we not count that as one of our many blessings?"

The two embraced and held each other for several seconds, neither saying a word but both feeling the depth of their connection. Katie then made each a Vodka Gimlet, and they later walked hand in hand to the porch and nestled side by side on the porch swing. The tart scent of lime filled the kitchen. As Asa and Katie sat silently enjoying another sunset, the twins scampered up and cuddled beside their parents. Katie looked down at her children, her heart swelling with love, as they seemed to understand the sacredness of the moment. Katie exhaled deeply, her voice soft and full of emotion, "Asa, there are no words to express how content and happy I am with our lives."

He turned to her, a small smile lifting the corners of his mouth. He squeezed her hand gently before looking back at the sky. "God's light has surely shown upon us. Just look at that sunset. I pray that when my time comes to leave this world, I will do so at sunset, with God's delicate and perfect image being the last etched upon my mortal eyes. If not, I fear my soul may explode from the shock of heaven's beauty."

Clover came through the den, where John sat by the fireplace, to retrieve some picture hanging wire from the kitchen. John said, "Cora just stopped by Clovie."

Clover paused mid-step, her head tilting slightly as a small smile spread across her face. "Really? It's been a while. Was it the dogs again?" John nodded, and Clover continued, "She loves animals and little children." His gaze drifted toward the fireplace as if seeing a memory flicker in the flames.

"She does," John replied.

Clover and John encountered Cora when they were very young, but their visits diminished as they grew older. John and Madie's children had similar experiences when they were young, as did the grandchildren in later years.

When Dottie was about four, she met Cora one afternoon while staying with her grandmother. As she sat on the floor combing a doll's hair, she looked to her right, and a girl about her size was sitting cross-legged with a brown teddy bear. Katie, again in the kitchen, heard the giggling and quiet conversation. Later, when she and Dottie were outside feeding the chickens, Katie asked her granddaughter, "Dottie, did someone come to play with you today?"

Dottie replied, "Yes, Cora played dollies with me! She had a teddy bear named Timmy." Katie just smiled and shook her head in amazement. Cora's teddy bear, "Timmy" was placed next to her in the casket.

As years passed, the apparitions came and went, and when an item would be misplaced or moved around the house, a typical response was, "Cora's up to mischief again."

Word soon got out around the farm that the Campbell house was haunted, a term the family never used. Haunted seemed unnatural and spooky, but nothing about Cora's visits was frightening. Her presence was gentle and familiar, like the warmth of memory that suddenly felt alive. The family just accepted it and went about their lives.

When John and Madie moved into Asa and Katie's home, the family took a group photo on the front porch one Christmas Eve. When the picture was examined, a blurred image of a small girl in what appears to be a blue dress with lace around the collar stood behind the sidelight window next to the front door. The family members stared in amazement. Naysayers say it's simply a glare from the sun's light reflecting from a porch column. However, the family knew otherwise. The shape, the size, the faint impression of lace – it was Cora. They didn't need proof; they had felt her presence for years.

# Chapter 21

**E**arly December through late January is duck season in Georgia, and Lake Early's northern shoreline is a favorite for local and visiting hunters. Bobby, Brooks, Alex, and their children are all avid duck hunters. While Georgia may not compare to the duck hunting experience found in Louisianna's or Arkansas' flooded rice fields, the hunting isn't bad if you know where to go. The Campbells primarily hunt on a remote, shallow section of the upper lake, only accessible by land or a long, dark boat ride from the nearest public launches. Since they own the land bordering the lake, there's little competition from other hunters, and the birds are plentiful. The family usually meets at Brooks' home for the early morning hunts when the air is crisp and biting at their noses and ears. They and the dogs load up in one or two boats and depart before sunrise. The boat rides are a mix of anticipation and nerves as they navigate stumps and cypress trees in the quiet darkness, the distant cries of geese and owls occasionally breaking the silence as the sun rises. The dogs pace in the boats eagerly, tails wagging furiously, their noses sniffing the air as if already catching the scent of the hunt.

Over a thousand acres of Campbell land is devoted to wildlife preservation, and several acres border the upper end of the lake and river. The land is home to whitetail deer, Eastern cottontail and swamp rabbits, turkeys, bobwhite quail, and several breeds of permanent and migratory wild ducks. John, Bobby, and Brooks have worked tirelessly to increase the quail numbers on their property, which has not been easy.

So much has changed since the bobwhite quail thrived in South Georgia, which began to see declines in the 1970s. The reasons for the decline of small game such as quail and rabbits are debated, but most agree that a shift in agricultural practices is partially to blame. In the 60s and 70s, most farms moved away from field terraces when larger tractors and cultivators came onto the scene. Terraces between cultivated strips in fields often grew up in bushy undergrowth, providing excellent cover for quail and rabbits. With the removal of terraces, so went the dense underbrush. In addition, invasive species such as fire ants, coyotes, and wild hogs have wreaked havoc on quail populations.

In the mid-80s, John Campbell partnered with state and national wildlife conservationists to develop a plan to build habitats for quail and rabbits. The progress was slow, but the numbers have rebounded, and several healthy coveys of wild quail now call the Campbell property home. South Georgia quail hunting with dogs is a tradition dating back to the farm's early days. The Campbells have used all types of bird dogs over the years, but the favorite is the English Pointer, which John calls the Cadillac of bird dogs.

For years, Brooks' barndominium was the sole structure on the acreage devoted to wildlife and hunting. Standing proudly amidst the wilderness, it feels like a sanctuary – a place where the grind of the outside world fades into the hum of nature. He built the home near the bank of a backwater slough on the upper end of Lake Early. Like most barndominium plans, it's half shop and half home. The shop or garage has room for two vehicles and a recessed area for a workshop and bathroom. The smell of engine grease and sawdust cling to the air, mingling with the faint, earthy aroma of the nearby water. Tools line the walls with precise care, each one a testament to Brooks' hands-on nature.

The house has a large downstairs kitchen and living room with a fireplace and half bath. The kitchen butcher block counters tell their own story, marked with knife scratches and a faint sheen from years of scrubbing. The living room, with its stone fireplace at the heart, embraces like a warm hug during wet Georgia winters. Upstairs is a large master bedroom with a bath and a second bedroom and bath. The bedrooms were simple but comfortable, with quilts hand-stitched by Brooks' mother still draped over the beds, adding a touch of nostalgia to the space. Outside, the home has a large wrap-around front porch with rough-sawn cypress posts with river-rock veneer at the bases supporting the roof structure.

Brooks' place is home to a small pack of hunting dogs the family uses for quail, duck and rabbit hunting. Each dog is more than just a hunting partner; they are family. Brooks often crouches by their kennels, scratching ears and murmuring encouragement, his voice low and calming.

The hunting dogs are housed in separate kennels with a shared two-acre fenced and cross-fenced run. The pointers, beagles, and retrievers are usually free to co-mingle with each other but can be separated if needed. Hank, the Scottie and Pearl, the border collie, are free-range and come and go as they please from Brooks' home through a pet door. Ask anyone who knows, and they'll tell you the Campbell Farm is an authentic Heaven on Earth for dogs and cats. Each pet is treated like family, and their healthcare is top-notch, with two- soon-to-be three veterinarians in the family. The animals don't just survive; they thrive, their every need met with care and love. You can see it in the shine of their coats and the eager way they greet anyone who crosses their path.

In addition to the dogs and a few cats, a pet cow calls Brooks' place home. MooDelle is a 26-year-old Red Angus that Brooks purchased from the local Sullivan County livestock barn. The barn conducts weekly cattle auctions on Thursdays, and Brooks usually attends.

MooDelle entered the sale ring, and the auctioneer announced, "Before I begin bidding on this cow, I'd like to make an announcement. This cow is 24 years old and has had 21 calves. This year is the first she's not calved. She's an old girl but looks healthy."

Brooks walked up to the ring and looked at the old red cow standing in the center of the ring. She stood still but looked around with wide eyes in an apparent state of confusion. The poor girl had likely never left the farm she was born on but now found herself in a strange place surrounded by strange eyes. Brooks held his hand up to stop the auctioneer before he began the bidding.

He said, "I don't know who brought this cow, and I don't want to know, but I'll be damned if I'll see her go to a slaughterhouse. She's given all she's got, and she deserves better than this."

He looked at the commercial buyers and said, "She's going home with me, boys, and she'll live out what time she has left on my farm." Bidding started, and Brooks was the sole bid. He brought

MooDelle home for $25. Today, MooDelle lives at Brooks' place in a three-acre fenced pasture with Jake's Quarter Horse, Randy. The two share a stable for staying warm and dry in inclement weather. They have become great pasture mates and are often let out of the small pasture to wander around the remote property.

Venomous snakes are plentiful in South Georgia, and snake bites are not altogether uncommon. The vet hospital treats several each year. Brooks' Scottie Hank was bitten by a large diamond back rattlesnake when he was just over a year old. Brooks came home for lunch from cutting hay. Upon walking onto the back porch, he was startled to see a large Diamond Back stretched out. Six inches of the snake's neck and head were removed and found lying next to the body. Pearl ran up playfully, apparently unharmed, but Hank wasn't around. Brooks went inside and found him under the kitchen table, alive but wheezing for air. He quickly but gently picked him up and laid him on the table. Brooks could smell and feel the venom on Hank's chest. Based on Dottie's previous instructions for animal shock, he grabbed a vial from the fridge and gave him .5 mL of epinephrine. Within seconds, Hank was on his feet and panting heavily. Brooks put him in the truck and sped to the vet hospital.

Dottie was in the middle of surgery, reconstructing a golden retriever's jaw from a car accident, but Clover was between exam rooms and had just wiped her hands on her scrubs when Brooks came in the back door with Hank. His face was pale, and his steps were quick as the door swung shut behind him.

"Hank fought a diamondback, but he's in a bad way," he said, his voice tight. Clover met him at an empty exam table, her lips pressing into a thin line as she took in his condition. She quickly started an IV and drew blood for testing. She then examined the front of Hank's chest and found two puncture wounds.

Her eyes widened slightly as she let out a low whistle. "Jesus, that must have been a big son-of-a-bitch. The fangs are over an inch apart!"

Brooks, his face tight with worry, gave a strained chuckle. He ran a hand through his hair and replied, "If it's not six and a half feet, I'll eat the damn thing raw."

Clover shaved the area around the bite and said, "Just an inch away from your carotid, Hankie Boy. You got lucky this time." She gently grasped his muzzle, bending her face close to his, and butterfly-kissed noses with him, "You're a tough little bastard." She murmured with a small, genuine smile.

Sadie Brown, the chief vet tech, walked up with the results from the snake bite test and said what was expected, "He's been envenomated."

Clover asked Sadie to start Hank on a round of antivenom and gently stroked Hank's head before easing him into a Kennel for treatment. "You are in good hands now, Hank." She mumbled under her breath.

Brooks walked over to watch Dottie wire a jaw together. He leaned on the edge of the doorframe, his arms crossed tightly against his chest as if bracing himself.

Dottie said, "That bite would have killed most dogs. Those damn Scotties are some tough characters. They'll recheck his blood following the first infusion to see if he needs another."

Brooks let out a heavy sigh, his shoulders slumping slightly, "That little shit's gonna end up costing me a fortune, but I suppose he's worth it. Hell, I may have to work it off up here mopping floors."

Dottie looked up from her task and rolled her eyes. "I'm sure your Aunt Clover will find a project for you at the house," she said.

Brooks raised his eyebrows and said, "Oh, how I know!"

# Chapter 22

In 2017, Clover and Dottie were approached by Brandon O'Donnell, a production scout for the Animal Channel. The network sought a rural vet practice in the south for a new yet-to-be-named reality series. O'Donnell had been given a tip regarding the Campbell Vet Hospital, farm, and brewery from a production assistant who grew up in the area but did not know the family personally. Once he did some digging online, he was interested in looking further, so he made arrangements to travel to Sullivan County.

O'Donnell stopped by the hospital late one afternoon before closing. The soft hum of fluorescent lights filled the mostly empty waiting room, and the faint scent of antiseptic lingered in the air. He was delighted to see the waiting room primarily empty. He approached the counter, introduced himself, and handed his card to Jessica Heard, the receptionist. She looked up with a polite nod; her neatly pinned name tag glinted under the overheard light. He apologized for stopping by without an appointment but hoped to catch Dr. Pierson and Dr. Simpson. Jessica glanced at the card briefly before meeting his eyes, "Dr. Clover, I mean, Pierson isn't working today," she said, her lips quirking a small apologetic smile, "But I'll let Dr Simpson know you're out here."

A few minutes later, the door to the back opened with a soft creak, and Dottie came to the front and introduced herself. The two shook hands, and Brandon informed her of his role and mission.

Dottie gave him a brief office tour, including the display of Doctor Dottie's food selections. They eventually ended up in Dottie's office, where she offered him a seat across from her desk. The office was cozy, with framed certificates lining the walls and a faint scent of lavender lingering in the air.

Brandon reviewed the details of what the network was looking for and said, "Dr. Simpson, I think your practice fits what we are looking for. From what I've been told, your family operates a farm and beer brewery."

Dottie nodded her head and said, "That's correct." She said. Her hands rested loosely on the desk, fingers interlaced as she spoke with pride. "My older brother is president of Schneider Brewery, and my younger brother runs the farm. My Aunt started this practice in the mid-70s after graduating from vet school. I joined her approximately 20 years later. My daughter Jenna will soon finish vet school and plans to join as well."

Brandon's eyes lit up, his brows lifting in surprise, "Wow, three generations in one practice! Your aunt, that's Dr. Velma Pierson?"

Dottie smiled, a hint of fondness in her expression, "Yes, but she goes by Clover. She's in her late 70s and works three days a week now. Another vet, Jeb McKinnley, and I are here full-time, and I have a couple of part-time doctors who cover vacations."

Brandon brought up the subject of the series, and Dottie leaned back slightly in her chair, her arms resting lightly on the desk as she respectfully listened to his pitch. Her brow furrowed in thought, and she occasionally nodded, indicating she was following along.

Once finished, she paused, her fingers tapping lightly on the desk, before she spoke, "Mr. O'Donnell, you've found us on an unusually slow day, but our practice is typically bustling and often loud and hectic. I'm not sure we have the bandwidth to handle the added stress of cameras and performing for an audience."

O'Donnell replied, "Please call me Brandon. I certainly understand your reluctance, but I assure you the filming isn't nearly as intrusive or as often as you might expect. The network has been doing this for a while, and the filming has evolved into a relatively seamless process."

Dottie tilted her head, a faint smile tugging at the corner of her lips, "Well, I'm not sure how these things work, and forgive me, but I watch very little TV and have never been fond of reality shows. They seem to be overly dramatic and staged."

Brandon chuckled softly, "No doubt that's the case with some shows. However, that's not what we are looking to do. Have you watched any of our series or programs?"

Dottie nodded and said, "Sure, I particularly enjoyed the series on the migratory patterns of hummingbirds last year, but I'm unaware of any reality shows on the network."

Brandon's face lit up, "Ah, the hummingbird series was a favorite of mine as well. You have good taste!" he paused, then added, "We only have one regular series that would classify as reality, Zoo Crew."

Dottie's lips curled into a small smile. She tilted her head as a flicker of recognition crossed her face, "I forgot about that one. I've seen it a couple of times. My daughter told me about it."

Brandon continued, "It's a light-hearted but informative show on the behind-the-scenes of two of the nation's top zoos. We make a concerted effort to keep our programs about animals and their welfare and not be overshadowed by humans, but we seek to promote the animal-person bond."

Dottie nodded in acknowledgment, and Brandon continued, "In addition to the practice and farm, I understand your family has set aside several acres for wildlife conservation."

Dottie acknowledged with another nod and offered, "My father, who is Clover- Dr. Pierson's twin brother, along with my brothers, have worked hard to reestablish some native species on several hundred acres of our family land. I've helped where possible, but they've put in all the hard work with my husband and two nephews."

Brandon's expression glowed with genuine admiration. "That's remarkable, Dr. Simpson." He leaned forward slightly, his voice warm, "With your permission, I'd like to share our discussion and my notes with our producers. If you and your aunt would be interested, I'm confident they would like to talk further with you."

Dottie stood and said, "I'll run this by Clover and my staff here, along with my family, and I'll be glad to talk further. Just stop by or call anytime."

Brandon shook Dottie's hand and left the practice as they closed for the day.

Once Brandon got in his rental and headed for the state park where he had rented a cabin, he called his Director of Programming,

Alan Kaplan. Brandon told Kaplan of the visit. Kaplan listened and gained interest as Brandon continued.

Brandon said, "Alan, I've spoken to many people here, and they all speak highly of the vet practice and the family in general. The Campbells operate a large brewery started by their ancestors over a hundred years ago. The brand is Schneider. I'd never heard of it before a few weeks ago when I happened to pick a six-pack up at my local bottle shop in Vegas. Have you heard of it?"

Kaplan's voice crackled through the line, his tone a bit curious. "No, I haven't, but I'm not much of a beer drinker. I'm pulling up their website now. It's a sizable operation."

Brandon glanced out the window, a slight smile tugging at his lips as he continued, "Oh yeah, far from a microbrewery. They're one of the largest privately owned breweries in the US." Alan let out a low whistle, "That's impressive. How was your introduction received?" Brandon briefed Alan on the conversation, his fingers tapping lightly on the steering wheel as he spoke, telling him that Dottie would be speaking with her family and staff but had agreed to further discussions. The call ended, but Brandon O'Donnell knew he'd found the perfect setting for the series.

Before Dottie left for the day, she told Sadie Brown about the conversation with O'Donnell and asked for her thoughts. Sadie, looking up from her desk and tapping her pen thoughtfully, considered for a few seconds and said, "Well, I don't see how it could hurt business. However, it may give your family more attention than you care to receive. You know I'll support anything you and Dr. Clover want to do, and it could be fun. I've always wanted to be a movie star!"

Dottie laughed, a lighthearted chuckle escaping her lips, "Yeah, I doubt it's something we will follow through with, but I'll run it by Clover and the guys."

The same week that O'Donnell visited Dottie, Libby Maddox received a call from a production scout asking about Schneider's interest in being in a show. Libby's eyes widened as she heard the offer, and she quickly jotted down the details, a slight thrill in her voice when she hung up. That Friday, the family gathered at the Pump House to discuss the events of late. Dottie sat back, her hands wrapped around a steaming mug, looking at each family member as they spoke. She had already filled Clover in on the visit with O'Donnell. Although Clover had given Dottie control years ago regarding the running of the practice, Dottie continued to seek her aunt's advice. Clover said she didn't care one way or the other as long as it didn't create more workload for the staff.

As the family settled into their chairs at the Pump House, Brooks nudged Clover and said, "Aunt Clover, you're gonna be a movie star!"

Clover smirked, a twinkle in her eye. "Hell, you too, Brookie. According to Dottie, he asked about the farm."

Brooks leaned back in his chair with a hearty laugh, crossing his arms and shaking his head, "Who the hell would tune in to watch the boring shit we do around here all day? Daddy, what do you think?"

John, sitting back in his usual spot, his fingers drumming on his beer bottle, "Did the topic of money come up?"

Dottie said, "Briefly, but he said the producers handled those discussions."

John, with his usual bluntness, said, "Well, as they say, money talks and bullshit walks."

Bobby, who had been quietly listening, asked Dottie, "Did he mention the brewery?"

She responded with a slight shrug, "Only in passing regarding our family. He did say he purchased a six-pack of Bock in Vegas, where he lives."

Bobby furrowed his brow, "Well, maybe it's a coincidence, but it seems unlikely since we both received requests the same week,"

Julie, ever the skeptic, leaned in, curiosity and suspicion evident in her eyes, "Which network called you, Hun?"

Bobby glanced at his phone, "I don't remember, but I'm texting Libby. She'll remember." Julie clearly not convinced, shook her head, "Doesn't sound like a coincidence to me- sounds like a coordinated attack. I've believed for years this was inevitable. This family is ripe for a TV show."

Bobby answered her earlier question, "Libby says it's the Cuisine Channel. It's a series called 'Beer, Proof God Loves Us and Wants Us to Be Happy.' I'll be damned. You all know I've got that quote framed in my office?"

Brooks said, "Yeah, Good Ol Ben Franklin! That's a cool title for a show."

As he looked at his iPhone, Joe said, "Both the Cuisine Channel and Animal Channel are on the same streaming service, so probably not a coincidence." He raised an eyebrow, glancing up from his phone as if expecting an answer.

Bobby continued, "I tell you what, the brewery could use a boost. We're doing okay, but the pressure is on from the micro-brews, and we're barely keeping a foothold up north and out west. We have a good story, but not many people know it outside our home turf. "I'm gonna listen to what they have to say." He sighed, rubbing his temple as if the weight of the challenge had just hit him.

Dottie said, "Yeah, I suppose it won't hurt to listen to their pitch. I told them I would speak with my family and get back in contact next week." She crossed her arms, her eyes narrowing slightly, thinking it through.

Brooks, often happy to defer to his older siblings, said, "I'm sure y'all will do what's best. If somebody wants to film my country ass on a tractor or ankle-deep in cow shit, fine with me." He shrugged causally, a grin tugging at the corner of his mouth.

Dottie joined Brandon O'Donnell and Alan Kaplan on a conference call the following week. While on the call, she inquired about Bobby's request the same week. Alan replied, "That's not a coincidence, Dr. Simpson. In addition to the show Brandon discussed with you, I'm also working on another project for the Cuisine Channel. The series will be devoted entirely to beer. After speaking with Brandon, I researched the Schneider brand and am very interested in including your family's Brewery in the pilot episode. I'm surprised I've never heard of the brand before."

Dottie said, with a warm smile, "Call me Dottie, please. We've been a regional beer for most of our history. It's only been in the last three or four years that the brand has expanded outside the South."

Alan replied, "Dottie, I want you to know I looked all over Phoenix, where I live, for a six-pack but struck out."

Dottie's eyebrows furrowed with a touch of concern, and she responded, "I'm not sure if we have a distributor in the Southwest, but I'll check."

Alan continued, "Dottie, have you had enough time to think about the series?"

She said, pausing briefly to gather her thoughts, "Yes, and we are open to discussing the idea further, but we have a few concerns and questions."

Alan, nodding thoughtfully, said, "That's certainly understandable. Would you mind sharing some concerns with me?"

Dottie said, "Sure. The primary concern at the vet hospital is the camera crew's disruption of our workflow. Another is loss of privacy and anonymity."

Alan responded, "The camera crew is almost always a crew of one. We also use mounted cameras placed overhead and out of the way. We try to use one camera person for a series as much as possible so they become familiar with the environment and the individuals being filmed. It's not as disruptive as you may think. Our camera crews know how to blend in and not be obtrusive. It's also not as often either. We don't film in person every day or even every week. We have the mounted cameras always recording unless you choose to turn them off for privacy reasons. Should something get filmed that you wish not to be shared, you can delete the recordings. We receive no recordings until you submit them at the end of the week, and you or your designee have complete control over content before airing.

If anyone, be it staff or a client, wishes not to be filmed, those wishes are granted. If they don't mind being filmed but choose to remain anonymous, we blur their faces for the episode. However, we find that most people do not object."

Dottie nodded slowly, absorbing the information, and then thanked Alan for the information and said, "You mentioned blurred faces. What about bleeping out words? My Aunt can out-cuss a sailor from time to time. She's an excellent veterinarian and has taught me so much, especially about surgery, but she has no filter."

Alan laughed and said, "This series targets adults, so profanity isn't necessarily an issue; however, if something is said that doesn't meet our ratings for the show, it is edited out or bleeped."

Dottie smiled at the thought and responded, "Thank you both for the call, but I'm being summoned out of my office, so we're going to need to wrap this up."

Alan said, "Thanks for your time, Dottie. I'd like to visit soon if that's okay with you and your family."

Dottie said, "That's fine, just give us a heads up."

After hanging up, Dottie stood up and stretched before leaving her office. She saw a few clients before breaking for lunch, and she and Clover walked over to the farm store, chatting causally. They each fixed a plate of meatloaf, mashed potatoes, and butterbeans, which Joyce had prepared, and sat on the back porch.

Clover said, "What did the Hollywood folks have to say?"

Dottie recapped the discussion and asked Clover for her thoughts. Clover said with a twinkle in her eye, "Honey, I'm all for promoting our brand. I mean, Jesus, if people tune in to watch that fat mama and her beauty queen daughter, they ought to love us. In my opinion, there's not much on TV these days worth a shit. Gone are the days of Carol Burnette, Lawrence Welk and Hee Haw. They just throw shit together for $3.99 per episode now, and the stupid American public watch it."

Clover took a bite of meatloaf and a swig of sweet tea and continued. "I'm sure there are some asshole vets out there who will critique and criticize my methods but ask me if I give a fiddlin' shit. I know what works and what doesn't." Dottie giggled at her aunt's honesty and said, "I feel the same way."

It didn't take long for Alan Kaplan to reach out to Dottie to request an in-person meeting. While on the phone, he said, "Dottie, I'm going to be honest with you here: I've never found a better setting for a series than your family. The brewery, vet practice, and farm are a producer's dream. Also, what's this I hear about a band?"

Dottie chuckled softly, her eyes lighting up at the thought, "That's just us having fun, but we put on a pretty good show. We're all musicians, and all sing. We have a gig at a local bar on the lake in three weeks."

Alan replied, grinning widely, "Is that right? Well, I would be delighted to attend."

Dottie said, "You're welcome to come."

"Do you mind if I bring my family?" Alan asked.

She nodded her head, "Sure, that's fine. Where will you be staying?

Alan shrugged, "Brandon stayed at the state park nearby, I believe."

Dottie said with a slight frown, "The state park just closed all accommodations for the season due to a remodel. You and your family are welcome to stay at our lake house."

Alan said, "That's certainly kind of you. I hope it's not a bother."

"Not at all, and there's plenty of room."

# Chapter 23

The Kaplans traveled to Georgia in late October to meet the Campbell family. Alan arrived at the vet office on Friday just before closing for a meeting with Dottie, Clover, and Sadie Brown. His wife, Jennifer and 15-year-old son, Henry, waited outside. Jennifer, leaning against the car with her arms crossed, gazing out over the horizon, while Henry fiddled with his phone, his eyes darting nervously between the screen and the entrance of the office. Alan went inside, his footsteps echoing on the tile floor as he took in the familiar environment. After introductions, they settled in the staff breakroom, the air filled with the faint scent of coffee and the hum of a nearby refrigerator.

Alan said, "I've spoken to Dottie at length over the phone a couple of times, but it sure is nice to meet each of you in person. So, how does everyone feel about being on TV?"

Sadie Brown was the first to speak up, her lips curving into a wide, eager smile as her hands rested on the edge of the table, almost as if holding herself back from bouncing in excitement, saying, "Good to meet you too, and I think we are all excited. You know, we really don't know what to expect. We just want to make sure the practice is cast in a positive light. Our vets are the best there is, and I'm proud to be able to show them off!" Her voice trembled with the excitement of someone who has been waiting for an opportunity like this for years.

Clover, who had been quietly observing, chimed in with a playful smile, tapping her fingers on the table rhythmically, her eyes twinkling with mischief, "Thanks so much for saying that, but just so you know, Alan, Sadie pretty much runs this place. She keeps Dottie, Jeb, and me on schedule and keeps this place running as smoothly as possible."

Alan nodded at the acknowledgment, a light chuckle escaping his lips as he glanced from Clover to Sadie, his eyebrows raised in impressed admiration. He said, "I bet she does. Sadie, you have my word that we intend to do just that." His voice softened, and his tone became more sincere, his gaze fixed on Sadie, "The Animal Channel will host this series, and we are committed to promoting the importance of the human and animal bond." There was a moment of silence, almost reverent, as everyone exchanged glances, the weight of Alan's word sinking in. A few questions and answers were exchanged, and the Kaplans soon headed to the lake house.

Dottie led them on the short trip from the vet hospital and got them settled in their weekend accommodations. As they approached the house, the trees surrounding the property stood tall like sentinels, their leaves tinged with the gold and red hues of fall, the air crisp with the scent of pine and earth.

Dottie said in the home's kitchen, "We've stocked a few essentials you folks may need for the weekend, but it's steaks tonight. The boys will be here soon to get the grills going, and I'll be back with my husband, Alex, as soon as I go home and change."

Alan and his wife Jennifer thanked Dottie for their hospitality and told her they looked forward to meeting everyone later.

After Dottie left, the family began to gather their things and got settled for the weekend. Their son, Henry, dashed upstairs, his feet barely touching the ground as he ran, his voice echoing back down the hall in excited bursts. His bag, a bit too big for him, bounced against his side as he reached the top of the stairs, his face lighting up as he looked at the different rooms.

Jennifer looked at Alan and said, "Well, it looks like there are plenty of bedrooms, so pick one as long as it's not mine." Alan stood silent, his expression softening with a flicker of uncertainty. His shoulder slumped slightly as if the weight of the situation was beginning to press on him. He looked at his wife with an expression that showed a man in defeat. A deep sigh escaped his lips as he glanced away, his eyes momentarily fixed on the floor, before slowly gathering his bag and walking upstairs.

Alan and Jennifer settled in their respective rooms. The house was quiet, and the cool, crisp air from the lake drifted through an open window. Henry, his excitement practically bubbling over, ran down the stairs, his sneakers thudding against the wood as he skidded around the corner. "This place is nice. Did you guys see the deer?"

Jennifer walked from her room and said, "Yes. It scared the shit out of me! I thought the damn thing was alive!"

Henry laughed and said, "I'm going outside to check out the lake."

Alan came from his room, his shirt slightly wrinkled from the long trip, the weight of the day's events hanging over him like a quiet storm. He tried making small talk with Jennifer, but she, already pulling away into herself, brushed him off with a quick glance. He paused, hesitating for a moment, then shrugged and followed Henry outside on the dock.

Henry said, "They have some fishing poles. I haven't been fishing in forever! I wonder if they have any bait."

Alan replied, "I'm sure they will set us up, son."

Jennifer stayed inside, her back to the cool glass of the window, her thoughts wandering in a way that they had far too often in recent years. She fixed herself a cocktail, the glass heavy in her hand, and took a slow sip. "What am I doing in bum fuck Georgia?" she thought, her eyes narrowing slightly as she looked out at the serene, almost haunting beauty of the lake. She stood in the kitchen alone, sipping her gin and tonic, until her eyes landed on Alan and Henry on the dock and reluctantly decided to join them. She walked along the lawn, drink in hand, and for the first time stopped to admire the beauty of the surroundings. As she peered across the lake, she exclaimed,

"Holy shit! Is that an alligator?" Alan and Henry turned to look as Jennifer pointed across the open lake. Sure enough, a six-foot gator swam slowly parallel to the lake shore a few yards from the dock.

Henry proudly declared, "Yes, it is! That's the first one I've seen in the wild. I didn't know they had them in Georgia!"

Alan chuckled, a mischievous glint in his eye. "Evidently, they do! Don't see those in Phoenix, do you, Henry!" Henry smiled and shook his head.

Jennifer, still processing the strange sight before her, asked, "People swim in this lake?"

Alan glanced at her with a shrug, his expression casual as if it was just another piece of strange information, "I guess so. There's a ladder off the dock into the water."

Jennifer walked to the dock to join her family; her drink now almost forgotten in her hand. As she approached, the gentle creak of the dock beneath her feet was the only sound besides the occasional distant bird call. She looked at Alan and Henry, who were still watching the alligator, their attention rapt. The afternoon light caught their faces, turning their looks into shadows of curiosity. And while they watched the alligator, Brooks and Jake appeared and walked across the lawn toward the dock. Henry saw them first and tapped his dad's shoulder. Alan turned and said, "Hi there. I can only assume you two are Campbells."

Brooks laughed, a deep, hearty laugh that seemed to echo off the water and said, "Guilty as charged. You must be the Kaplans. I'm Brooks, and this is my son Jake."

Alan, Jennifer and Henry walked up to meet the guys and exchanged handshakes. Henry said, "We just saw an alligator!"

Brooks smiled, "Yeah, I bet. No shortage of those in Lake Early- or the river."

Alan said, "Jennifer was just asking me if you guys swim in the lake."

Brooks, who was already making himself comfortable in the conversation, nodded, "Sure we do. Everyone does. The gators are mostly harmless. They have been known to take a small pet occasionally, but even that is rare. There's plenty of food for them in the lake, and they are naturally skittish. Speaking of food, son, would you head up to the lodge and lay out several steaks for tonight?"

Jake replied, "Sure, Dad. Henry, come on." The boys trotted to the lodge, their sneakers crunching on the gravel as they made their way inside. They retrieved the steaks from the freezer, the cold air hitting them as they pulled out the packages, the smell of fresh meat hanging in the air.

Henry, with a hint of curiosity in his voice, asked, "Jake, do you guys have some bait I can use to fish?"

Jake, always ready for an adventure, grinned. "We have a spot where you can get worms. I'll show ya. You can catch some bream, crappie, and catfish off the dock. There's a tackle box and fishing poles in the boat house. I'll tell you what, let's put some lines out now." Henry's eyes widened. "Hell yeah!" Jake laughed and led him back to the boat house.

As they neared the boathouse, Jake noticed two boats approaching where their parents were gathered. Jake motioned in the direction and said, "Dad, look." Brooks and the others turned to see a small boat approaching, followed by a Georgia Game Warden's boat.

Brooks grinned and said, "Folks, this should be good. Allow me to introduce our farm manager, Jamey Jones, who is being escorted by Lake Early's finest, a Georgia Game Warden, or as I refer to them, the 'Paw Patrol.' Fair warning- Jamey has the vocabulary of a drunk frat boy. I refer to him as 'Muthafucker Jones.' You will soon see why."

Jake giggled and said, "Yep, sure will."

As Jamey's small boat approached, he yelled to Brooks. "Can you believe this muthafucka? I'm out here minding my own, fishing for crappie*," his voice raised, and he turned to the game warden –* "in John Campbell's canoe, and the rabbit policeman says the registration is expired. Registration for a muthafuckin canoe! What a crock of horse shit!"

Donnie Davis, the game warden, said, "Mr. Jones. I've told you the law says any motor-powered vessel must be registered. In addition, you've been drinking, and I could also cite you for indecent exposure for relieving yourself in public."

Jamey placed his right hand to his heart and said, "Guilty as charged officer! I was operating a canoe under the influence and took a piss off the side in the Thronateeska River! Mutherfucka and furthermore! Indecent exposure? Who the hell said it wasn't decent?" Brooks, Jake, Alan, Jennifer, and Henry could hardly compose themselves with laughter. The whole situation was absurd, and Jamey's unapologetic defiance only made it more comical.

When Jamey's boat arrived at the dock, Jake grabbed a rope and tied it to a cleat. Jamey gave him an exaggerated salute, "Thank you for securing my vessel, Baby Jake."

Jamey turned to the game warden and said, "Officer, permission to go ashore, or shall you handcuff me here?"

Davis, his patience wearing thin, responded, "Just put the damn sticker on the boat." Brooks laughed and said, "Thanks, Donny. I'll take care of it. Damn thing is probably in Daddy's truck." Davis nodded and sped away.

Jamey saw Jennifer and said, "Forgive me, madam. I didn't see you earlier. My apologies for the language."

Jennifer laughed and said, "Oh, no need to apologize. 'Motherfucker and furthermore.' I'm using that one!" Jamey threw back his head and laughed heartily, "Well, I'm certainly glad I didn't offend anyone."

Alan said, "No way, not in my family. I believe Henry's first word was 'fuck' from hearing it from his mother so much."

Jennifer elbowed Alan's side, looked at Henry, and said, "He hears it equally from both of us."

Henry, caught in the middle of his parents' banter, just rolled his eyes and smiled.

Brooks said, "Well, you folks will fit in just right with the Campbell crowd."

Soon after Jamey's brush with the law, the remaining Campbells arrived, including Rooster, Sally, and Vic Reynolds. Introductions were made with the Kaplans, and Bobby soon had the grill ready for steaks. Alan and Jennifer were treated like lifelong friends and made to feel at home. Henry joined Jake on the dock, where cast lines were baited with red wigglers. The Kaplans were immediately impressed at the apparent closeness and love this group had for each other.

Alan listened in, leaning casually against the counter as Vic and Clover conversed about his latest trip to the vet hospital with his Yorkie, Trixie.

Vic said, "Clover, did you see that mangy dog Rudisel Spivey had in the office Wednesday?"

Clover laughed, her lips curling into a grin, "No, I think Jeb took the honors."

Vic rolled his eyes, and continued, "He came in the lobby and sat next to me and Trixie, wearing that stupid cowboy hat as big as the hood on your Lincoln. I swear, he looked like an emaciated rabbit sitting under a collard leaf." Vic turned to Alan and said, "Rudisel has a dog ranch a few miles from here. He takes in strays and tries to find homes, but I think he keeps most."

Alan said, "That's nice. I guess it keeps them from going to the animal shelter."

Vic scoffed, shaking his head, "Yeah, I suppose so, but from the looks of that place, I may prefer the pound if I were a dog. He has money, but his damn place looks like a war zone. He rides around with several dogs in a beat-up piece of shit Hyundai, wearing that big-ass cowboy hat. It ought to be damn law- you can't drive a Hyundai and wear a cowboy hat."

Alan laughed and thought to himself, *"This is entertaining."*

Alan asked Vic how long he had known the Campbells. Vic grinned widely, his eyes glinting with nostalgia, "All my damn life. John, Clover, and I were in the same grade throughout school. Clover and I have always been best friends."

Clover, giving Vic a playful nudge, added, "Yeah, we go way back, don't we, old boy?" Vic leaned toward her, his voice softening with affection, "We sure do, sweetheart."

Before long, the men were gathered around the grill, each holding a bottle of Schneider. Julie said to Dottie, Amy, and Jennifer, "Come on, girls, let's go inside and see if we can find something stronger to mix up than just a salad."

Jennifer smirked, a twinkle in her eye, "Oh, I've already found the gin stash."

Dottie, laughing, raised an eyebrow. "A fellow gin drinker, huh?"

As they entered the second floor living room of the home, Jennifer replied, "Quite so, and more than usual lately, I'm afraid to say."

Julie replied, "Well honey, sometimes that's the way it goes. That asshole Bobby Campbell drives me to drink on a regular basis." A few chuckles followed. The ladies gathered around the island after mixing their cocktails, and each assisted with cutting up vegetables for the salad.

Jennifer, her fingers lightly trembling as she sliced the cucumber, said to the others, "It's certainly nice of you to put us up this weekend. I almost didn't come, but I'm so glad I did. Henry begged me, so I decided to join at the last minute. I'm sure it's the alcohol loosening inhibitions, but things haven't been the best in the Kaplan household lately." She stopped mid-sentence, feeling a flush of guilt, and apologized. "I'm sorry, ladies, we only just met, and here I am, bringing my drama all the way from Arizona."

Dottie, her expression warm and understanding, placed a hand on Jennifer's shoulder. "Jenn, no apology needed. We all have our struggles." Jennifer stared at the cucumber she was cutting and noticed her hands had begun to tremble. Her chest tightened, and tears stung in her eyes. She looked up and said, "The bastard cheated on me!" Her voice cracked, the raw emotion breaking through the mask she had worn for so long.

Julie and Dottie both stood next to her and offered warm embraces. Jennifer composed herself, and they quietly finished the salad, took their drinks to the living room and settled on the sectional leather sofa. Julie and Dottie allowed Jennifer to talk, and she explained how she had recently learned of Alan's affair with a young assistant.

Dottie said, "Darlin, it happens to the best of us. Alex and I went through this about five years ago when he ran around on me with a coworker. I was devastated. Nothing compares to it, not even losing my mother." She paused, shaking her head at the memory. "I hated that son of a bitch, and we split for a couple of weeks. I was so torn. My family wasn't much help aside from Julie and Amy. Both the boys and Daddy wanted to kill him and didn't offer me much in the way of compassion."

Amy, her voice dripping with bitterness, added, "Well, certainly not Brooks. God knows he can't keep his dick in his pants."

Dottie nodded in agreement and continued, "After the first couple of weeks, I allowed Alex back in. He was brokenhearted as well and begged me a thousand times to forgive him. It was a tough few months, but we got through it. For me, I had to decide if he was worth it as a husband to me and a father to Jenna. I'm not a quitter, and so I decided what we had was worth fighting for. So the only question for you is, Is Alan worth fighting for?"

Jennifer looked up at the ceiling. Her heart was clenched, torn between anger and love. She took a deep breath and replied, "He is. The son of a bitch is."

Dottie's gaze softened, but there was strength in her words, "Well, that's your answer then. Do whatever it takes to get it back on track. I'm not making excuses for them, and I've told that long-legged Alex Simpson if he ever does this again, I'll cut his damn balls out just like I have for a thousand dogs and cats, but they rarely look at sex the way we women do. They just aren't as evolved."

Julie replied, "Amen, sister. If you really want to know the truth, sex to them is one notch above jacking their dicks. Fact is, we're sacred creatures compared to those knuckle-dragging apes."

Jennifer chuckled and said, "That's the damn truth!" Amy's phone buzzed, and she informed the others, "Brooks says steaks are ready. I'll get the salad from the fridge."

As the ladies went outside, Bobby announced, "Steaks are ready. If you want anything other than medium-rare, the grill is still hot, so have at it, but I'll not disrespect the memory of this steer by overcooking it."

As the group ate, Jennifer commented on the tenderness and flavor of the steak. "This steak is delicious. What did you season it with? Or is that a family secret?"

Bobby replied, "No secret, just a little garlic salt and black pepper." Jennifer looked surprised, raising an eyebrow. "Really? I would have thought it was marinated in something." Brooks replied this time. "It's tasty because of how the cow is finished off."

Brooks smiled, seeing the confusion on her face. "Finishing is how the animals are fed in the last stages before slaughter. The large feedlots, where most beef is finished, feed 75-90% grain and soybean meal and 10-25% cottonseed meal for three to six months. While this adds weight to the animal more rapidly, it also dulls the taste, in my opinion." He paused to let the information sink in before looking at Jennifer, whose face was still wrinkled in thought. "We keep our cattle on grass until 90 days before slaughter. We finish our cattle with limited grazing on grass, clover and feed, including waste products from the brewery called brewers' grain." He shrugged casually as if it were no big deal, but there was a certain pride in his voice.

Alan echoed his wife's admiration for the steak- "I've been in some fancy steakhouses before, and this is as good or better."

After supper, Rooster walked down to the lakefront, where Henry and Jake resumed fishing. Alan soon joined them, and he and Rooster walked along the shoreline, leaving the boys behind.

Alan asked, "Rooster, how long have you known the Campbells?"

Rooster replied, "All my life. I was born on the Campbell Farm. My Daddy and granddaddy worked for the Campbells, and I followed in their footsteps. Along the way, John and I became the best of friends." Rooster detailed their lifelong friendship and his and Sweet's involvement in the Campbell Foundation. He continued, "They're rough around the edges- those Campbells. They cuss more than any white folks I know, but they have done more than you can imagine for people around these parts- black, white, or Mexican. It would take all night for me to list the families they have helped. Hell, John, Madie, and Clover paid for my boy Grady's college and medical school. That boy's education didn't cost me and his mama one dime, and we ain't the only ones they've done that for. That's why they are loved so much around here."

Alan replied, "What a wonderful family legacy." He smiled, deeply moved by Rooster's words.

As Rooster and Alan's conversation continued, Brooks walked up and said, "Alan, Uncle Remus isn't divulging any dark family secrets, is he?"

Alan, with a glint of mischief in his eyes, replied, "Just a few."

Brooks smiled and said, "Alan, this fellow is like another father to me and Sweet like my mama. They helped raise us just like Aunt Clover."

Alan smiled and said, "I bet they did. Looks like you kids had a bunch of people looking out for you."

Rooster tilted his head in Brooks' direction and said, "Yeah, and it still wasn't enough eyes to keep his crazy ass straight." Brooks smiled in knowing recognition at Rooster's comment. He said, "Yeah, Mama always said her baby was a little bit crazy."

Brooks looked toward the house and the others and said, "Looks like Daddy has his fiddle out. I guess we better get back up there."

As the men joined the others around the fire pit, Vic Reynolds motioned for Joe to hurry up with the keyboards. "Damn, boy. I could have driven to my house and back by now. What took you so long?" He sounded frustrated but amused, tapping his foot in impatience. Vic then saw Blake exiting the first floor of the lodge. He said, "Oh, now I get it! You two know we have guests here tonight." Joe smiled, and Blake blushed. As she passed by Vic, she whispered jokingly into his ear, "Now Vic, you know sometimes you just can't wait!" Vic bellowed, gave Joe a thumbs up and followed the young couple as they joined the rest of the group.

Alan said, "I didn't know we were having a concert." Vic was busy setting up the keyboards and said, "This crowd rarely gets together without some music. We thought we'd practice a few before tomorrow night." Alan found a seat and was pleased when Jennifer sat down next to him.

Bobby and Brooks got their guitars tuned, and Bobby picked out the instrumental to "She Talks to Angels" by the Black Crows on his Martin. Brooks strummed along and covered the vocals. Alan kept his eyes on Brooks but leaned toward Jennifer and said, "Did you tell them this was a favorite of mine?"

She shrugged and said, "I may have mentioned something. I can't recall."

The song ended, and Alan and Jennifer offered a standing ovation. Alan's hands were warm from clapping, and Jennifer's face was flushed with admiration.

Jennifer said, "I've never heard that song done any better!" Brooks took a gracious bow, and soon John Campbell began the intro to "Wagon Wheel" with his father's fiddle. Vic played piano while Bobby played along on his Martin and Brooks on harmonica. Bobby took the lead vocals, and when the song ended, another standing ovation by the Kaplans. The energy around the fire was electric, the applause ringing in the cool night air.

Dottie and Jenna walked up to Brooks, and Jenna said, "Now we can't let the boys have all the fun, can we, Mama?"

Dottie said, "Hell naw baby!" Bobby had his electric Les Gibson guitar tuned up and began the into, with Vic on the keyboard, to Fleetwood Mac's "You Make Loving Fun." Jenna sang lead while Dottie and Brooks sang back up, and at the song's completion, they moved into "Gypsy," where Dottie sang Stevie Nick's lead vocals. Her voice was hauntingly beautiful, a perfect match for the song. Vic had the keyboard just right, applying the organ and piano pieces flawlessly while Bobby played the guitar.

The next song in the Campbell Band lineup was "Me and Bobby McGee." John played the Martin, Bobby the Les Gibson, Clover at keyboards, and Brooks on harmonica. Brooks began the intro, and Clover sang the tune accompanied by John on a few lines, but Clover covered most of the song.

During the song, Alan discreetly asked Jennifer, "Can you believe this family? I've never been so fucking impressed in my life!" His voice was full of admiration, his gaze lingering on the Campbells as they played. She acknowledged with a nod, and they both listened as John sang the final verse. Once the song ended, Alan and Jennifer again offered their praise.

Brooks said, "Thanks so much, folks. It's not often we get such distinguished Hollywood guests around here."

Alan said, "Oh no, no! No Hollywood here, my new friend. Far from that." Alan reminded Brooks that he lived in Phoenix.

Rooster, Sweet, John, Clover, and Vic departed for home, leaving the younger Campbells with the Kaplans. Jenna, Andy, Joe, and Blake were down by the lake with Jake and Henry. Bobby, Julie, Alex, Dottie, Brooks, and Amy sat by the fire with the Kaplans and enjoyed the clear fall evening.

Alan addressed the group, "Folks, I don't mind saying I've never been so impressed! You guys are so talented."

Jennifer said, "You guys are amazing! You should go on the road."

Bobby took a bow, "Thanks, that means a lot. I think we'll just stick around here for now. We'd probably kill each other if we were cooped up on a tour bus."

Brooks shrugged, "There's not much I enjoy more than playing music with my family, but I sure wouldn't want to do it for a job. Jobs have a way of sucking the joy out of everything."

Alan replied, "Well, I can't argue with that." He continued, "Speaking of jobs, you all know what mine is and why we came here this weekend. What began as an idea of showcasing Dottie and Clover's vet practice on our Animal Channel has evolved into something much more comprehensive." He paused to gather his thoughts, his tone serious but optimistic.

"When Brandon O'Donnell phoned me after he visited the practice and met Dottie, I admit I did some digging on your family. We would like to build a series around the Campbells. The vet practice, the brewery, the farm, and last but not least, the band."

The Campbell siblings and their partners listened patiently, allowing Alan to continue. "Your family is extraordinary and has a beautiful story to tell. So much reality TV is scripted for dramatic effect and conflict, but that's not what we are looking to do. Have you had the opportunity to look over any of the documents I sent last week?" Kaplan referred to a sample contract the network sent to the family for review.

Bobby answered, "Yes, and we gave it to our attorney, Chuck Langdon. He will be here tomorrow to join any further discussions. However, as it stands, we will not move forward unless we are paid residuals. That is 100% non-negotiable."

Kaplan lowered his head and said, "Unfortunately, that's not a practice in reality TV." Bobby replied, "Well, that's fine. Nobody here is looking for a job. Our family is set if we never work again. Still, there's no way we intend for our likenesses or businesses to be used without residuals- in perpetuity. As Daddy says, 'Money talks and bullshit walks.' No disrespect intended, but we didn't come looking for you. You came to us. We will be fine; nobody here wants to be a celebrity anyway. We are only considering this for the opportunities it could bring to our community."

Alan replied, "I didn't say no. I just said it's not a typical practice, but have your attorney draw up what you think is fair, and I'll send it up the chain. I've been doing this for nearly 20 years now, and I know when I've found a show, and I'm telling you- America will eat the Campbells up!"

# Chapter 24

The following day, Brooks picked up Jennifer and Alan and took them on a tour of the farm operations. His truck rumbled over the dirt road, leaving a light cloud of dust in its wake as Jennifer and Alan climbed in, exchanging excited glances. They visited the cattle pastures and meat packing plant and rode by several hundred acres of barley in its early stages of growth. The young barley swayed gently in the morning breeze, glistening under the sun.

Jennifer commented, "That's the greenest field I've ever seen."

Brooks glanced at her with a satisfied nod, "We've been blessed with some good rain this October, so we haven't needed to irrigate. Irrigation keeps it alive, but nothing does what rain can." He explained, his hands lightly gripping the steering wheel.

Alan, always curious, pointed toward the fields, "Is this all used for the brewery?"

Brooks answered, "100%, and that's still not enough. We have two other farmers locally that we buy barley from as well."

As the truck jostled over a bump, Alan furrowed his brow. "What types of fertilizers do you guys use?"

Brooks exhaled, his face shifting into a thoughtful expression, "Well, I'd love to say we are 100% organic, but we haven't found the yields we need without commercial applications such as liquid nitrogen. We've used hundreds of tons of chicken litter for fertilizer, which is organic, but the poultry growers are applying compounds these days to cut back on ammonia emissions from growing houses. That, in turn, reduces the nitrogen, so it just doesn't work like it once did." Alan nodded, absorbing the information, while Jennifer gazed out at the endless sea of green, the sunlight dancing on the dew-kissed blades of barley.

Soon, Brooks pulled up at John and Clover's home for a brief tour.

As Clover conducted the tour, she stopped and pointed at a painting of Asa and Katie Campbell. Clover said, "That painting was done when Mama and Daddy were in their 60's." She smiled as her fingers lightly grazed the frame, "John and I were both still home. I think we were in the 9th or 10th grade." Jennifer leaned in, examining the fine details of the painting. "It's beautiful," she murmured, imaging the lives lived within the walls of this home. Clover smiled wistfully before gesturing toward portraits displayed in the main hall, including the Schneiders, Youngs, Thomas, and Cora.

"These are the Schneiders, the Youngs, and Thomas and Cora. Family ties run deep here."

Alan and Jennifer met Brooks' dogs, Hank, and Pearl, the night before, and as they returned to the living room were soon introduced to John and Clover's dogs, Daisy and Jack. Alan petted Jack on the head as Daisy, in typical Scottie fashion, seemed aloof and disinterested in the guests but respectfully walked up and offered a head to pat. Alan asked If everyone in the family owned a border collie and Scottie.

"Pretty much." Clover replied with a laugh, "Those two breeds have been on this farm all our lives. John and I received two Scotties one Christmas when we were six- a black boy and a wheaten girl. Mother named them Scotch and Soda. They were litter mates, and we had them for 14 years. They died within two weeks of each other." Her voice softened, and her eyes glimmered with the weight of bittersweet memories.

Jennifer said, "That is so sweet!"

Clover said, "They were precious souls. John and I were both still home. He was working for Daddy, and I was in nursing school. We weren't kids anymore, but losing them made us feel like we were all over again. We were heartbroken when those two left us. Mom came in and found that we had cried ourselves to sleep on my bed. She tucked us in at 20 years old, as she had done countless times before. It was one of those memories you never forget – bittersweet, a perfect blend of loss and love. They are buried out back in our family cemetery. One side is pets, the other, their owners."

Alan asked, "Would you mind showing us?"

Clover responded, "I'd be delighted."

As they continued the inside tour, Clover said, "The girls and I will soon be decorating the home for Christmas."

Jennifer said, "I bet it's beautiful."

Clover replied, "Julie is an interior decorator, so we all follow her orders. She has this uncanny ability to transform the house into something straight out of a Christmas movie."

The group walked to the back porch, and John led them to the family cemetery. The crisp air seemed to carry the faint scent of pine, mingled with the earthy aroma of fallen leaves. The area is approximately 50 X 50 feet, located between two elderly Live Oak trees and surrounded by a rock wall with one entrance facing east. They visited the graves of Karl and Karoline Schneider, Jack and Julia Young, Asa, Katie, Cora, and Madie Campbell. Each grave marked with a simple granite headstone. Jennifer stopped at Asa and Katie's grave, and noticed the dates of death, both in their mid to late 90's passing only a day apart.

John saw her staring at the gravestones and walked up. "Mama and Daddy left this world together in 1987." Jennifer looked at him with a look of compassion tinged with confusion. John's eyes narrowed slightly as he stared at his parent's headstones. "They were on their way home from the Piggly Wiggly in Collinsboro when a dump truck pulled in front of their path just two miles from here. Mama died instantly at the scene, and Daddy just after midnight the next day. It was tragic losing them like that, but God knows they would have wanted nothing more than to leave this world together." John paused and a gentle smile began to build as he thought of his loving parents. He continued, "The only family member missing is our older brother Thomas, who was killed during the war. He's buried in the Ardennes in Belgium." His voice softened, and for a brief moment, he stared at the ground as if speaking of Thomas brought the loss of the brother he never knew flooding back. The lines on his face deepened with a quiet, unspoken grief.

Alan found Scotch and Soda's paw-shaped headstones. He crouched down to trace the engraving with his fingers, his brow furrowing in concentration. "Scotch and Soda," he murmured as if saying their names made their presence a little more real. The pet's graves were marked with smaller granite headstones in the shapes of hearts, paws, and bones. Brooks pointed out Riley's grave with a bone-shaped headstone and said, "That old boy right there was one fine dog. He saw me go from kindergarten to college. Dad has a picture of him and me in cap and gown at kindergarten and high school graduations. The old boy made it to 16. That's a long time for a Scottie. We were big buddies. That joker went everywhere with us."

He paused, his voice thickening slightly, as he added, "I still catch myself expecting to see him waiting at the door sometimes." He then went on to tell the story of the trip out west. He continued, "I tell you, it's like a family member when one goes. We sure love our critters around here."

Jennifer said, "That's obvious. This place is so sweet and sacred."

Brooks said, "It's a special place for sure. I come up here sometimes at sunset, smoke a little weed or do some shrooms, meditate, play my harmonica, and let my family's spirits speak to me."

He smiled a little sheepishly, adding, "I know it sounds crazy, but it feels like they are still here, you know? Like they are watching over us."

Alan said, "That sounds like heaven." He glanced around the cemetery, his hands resting on the cool stone wall as if grounding himself in the history surrounding him.

The Kaplans and Brooks left John and Clover and rode to Brooks' home, where they met several more dogs and cats. They loaded up in Brooks' Jeep and toured the nearby property. Over 20 miles of primitive roads and trails cover the Campbell's land used for hunting and wildlife preservation, making it feel like a sprawling, untamed sanctuary. The air smelled of pine and damp earth, while the crunch of gravel under the Jeep's tires added a rhythmic backdrop to their journey. .

They first came to a section of bottom land near one of Lake Early's many sloughs. Brooks parked the Jeep. Alan and Jennifer joined him as he exited and walked among the trees near the water's edge. The stillness of the slough was broken only by the faint rustling of leaves and the occasional splash of a fish breaking the surface.

Brooks pointed out several mushroom species growing from the tree trunks and said, "I started inoculating trees with mushroom spores a few years ago."

He took his Case knife from his pocket and cut an outgrowth from a sweetgum tree. "This is called chicken of the woods. It's great for cooking. Like a portabella in texture, but actually taste like chicken." He then showed them some Shiitake specimens and said, "I've got mushrooms growing all over this place. We sell some in the store. They've become a local favorite."

Jennifer asked, "So, you grew these?"

Brooks said, "Yeah, I guess. I ordered the mushroom plugs, which are small wooden pegs coated with spores from various species. It's easy; you just drill a hole, insert the peg and cover it with wax. Takes a few months to see any fungus, but they'll produce for a couple of years."

Alan said, "Wow, you're quite the mushroom expert. What's that called? A mycologist?" Brooks laughed and said, "Hardly. My mother was really into nature and, what's it called? Foraging? Yeah, Mom was a flower child from the '60s and 100% hippie. She used to say that the earth gives us everything we need if we know where to look. I've got a lot of hippie in me, too."

He looked at the couple and asked, "Has anyone told you how they met?"

Both shook their heads, and Brooks continued. He leaned back against the Jeep, crossing his arms as if settling into a favorite story, "Dad was stationed at Edwards Air Force Base in the 60's. My grandparents had already laid one son on the altar of this country, and they didn't intend to repeat that, so Dad joined the Air Force instead of the Army, where he would have likely ended up in a Vietnamese jungle. He was in the reserves but called up to active duty in '65 and landed a pretty sweet assignment at Edwards. He went on a few missions to Vietnam, but only in a supply function. He said he spent a good bit of his time high as hell, but that's Dad for ya." Brooks added with a chuckle, shaking his head. "While at Edwards, he met Mom one weekend on leave in San Diego. Dad said their eyes met, and he knew that girl was special. Mom was in her first year of college working toward her teaching degree and was serving tables at a waterfront restaurant during the summer."

Jennifer tilted her head, "Was your mother from California?"

Brooks replied, "Pretty much. Her father was in the navy and sailed out of San Diego. She moved there when she was in grammar school. My grandparents were originally from Texas, and that's where Mom was born. She loved the ocean, though, and always said the waves had a way of washing away whatever was weighing her down." He picked up a small stick and turned it over in his hands, his voice quieter now, "Anyway, Mom was really into this kind of thing, and she got me interested in growing mushrooms. I studied a lot of plant biology in college as well, but mostly, I'm just curious. It's hard to explain, but it's like mushrooms were her way of staying connected to the earth. She believed they were proof of how life can spring from decay. It was something she and I did together that nobody else in the family took an interest in, so I kept at it. And honestly, I kinda feel like she's here with me in a sense. Every time I see one pop up, it's like she's saying, 'Hey Brookie. You behaving yourself?'" He smiled faintly, his fingers tightening on the stick for a moment before tossing it away. A few seconds of silence followed.

Brooks smiled, looked at Jennifer and Alan, and said, "I have some magic mushrooms growing too, but I don't sell those."

Alan chuckled, leaning back against the Jeep door and crossing his arms, "I don't blame you. You gotta keep the good stuff for yourself. God, I haven't done shrooms in years, not since Jenn and I were in college."

Brooks replied, "I microdose almost every day but take a trip or two a month." His tone turned serious as his expression changed to one of frustration tinged with disgust. He ran a hand through his hair and let out a sharp exhale, "Psilocybin mushrooms are so misunderstood in our culture, and it's not by accident." He said, his voice rising slightly with passion. He gestured emphatically, his hands moving like he was shaping the air around him. "Fucking big pharma controls congress at the state and federal level. They can't let the people heal naturally because where's the fucking money in that? It's a damn disgrace that so many people suffer aimlessly when God has given them what they need in nature." Brooks paused and shook his head as if trying to dispel the anger building within him. His lips pressed in a thin line, and he turned away for a moment, staring into the distance. "Sorry folks, It's just something I'm passionate about."

Jennifer gave a small, understanding smile and placed a hand on his arm, "No apology needed." She said warmly, and Alan nodded in agreement. They continued their journey and soon were back at Brooks' house, where they switched vehicles and headed to the Farm Store for lunch.

The cozy dining area smelled of rich, Southern cooking. They dined on fried chicken with white gravy, black-eyed peas, turnips, and cracklin' cornbread.

Brooks said, "Hope y'all like soul food." Jennifer and Alan offered their compliments, and Alan said, "God, if I spent much time down here, I'd gain 50 pounds."

Brooks laughed, wiping his hands on a napkin, "Yeah, Miss Joyce can fatten a fence post with her cooking." He said, leaning back in his chair with a satisfied sigh, "I guess our next stop is the brewery. Bobby is meeting us to give y'all a tour, so I suppose we need to head over."

After lunch, Brooks and the Kaplans took the short hop over to the brewery, where Bobby was waiting on the front porch of the original building. He raised a hand in greeting, the weathered boards creaking under his boots as he stepped forward. The three joined Bobby on the front porch, where a row of rockers were scattered along the length. Alan and Jennifer were immediately charmed by the old building. Alan admired a few vintage Schneider Beer tin signs from another time and asked, "Are these original?"

Bobby answered," We have some originals inside where they're protected from the elements. These are all reproductions we've had made based on the originals."

Jennifer nodded, glancing around, "As we pulled up, Brooks told us this is the original building."

Bobby responded, "It is. We've spent a fortune over the years preserving it. We could have saved a lot of money tearing the old girl down and rebuilding, but where's the legacy in that?"

Alan clapped Bobby on the back, "Exactly." He said with a nod of approval.

Bobby led them inside, where Alan and Jennifer both felt as if they had stepped back in time. Jennifer immediately noticed the old pine flooring with its prominent knots and wide grain pattern. The original golden hue had turned to cinnamon, and a few dents and scratches from over a hundred years of foot traffic displayed timeworn elegance. Bobby said, "The original brewhouse is used for offices and meeting spaces now, but it's still the heart of the property. Bobby then led the group on a short tour of the brewery facilities, describing each step along the way, from milling, malting, fermenting and conditioning.

Bobby described how the brewery runs 24/7 and rarely shuts down. "We've expanded the operation over the years, but the process is largely unchanged.

Alan couldn't help but be drawn to the energy of the place, his gaze sweeping over the workers. He was impressed by how friendly the staff was and how happy they seemed to work on a Saturday. He finally asked, curiosity edging his voice, "Bobby, what shifts do the employees work?"

Bobby replied, "We run two shifts, 7:00 AM to 7:00 PM. Employees switch from nights to days every six months and vice versa. Four days on and three days off one week and three days on and four days off the next."

The tour ended back at the brewhouse near Bobby's office, and the group gathered in a nearby conference room, where they found the rest of the Campbell family. Alan noticed paintings of Karl Schneider, Jack Young, and Asa Campbell hanging on the wall, lit by a lamp from above. Alan leaned in slightly, his fingers brushing the surface of the table, and said, "So these guys started it all, huh?"

John, who had been standing near the window, gave a slight nod and a knowing smile, his eyes gleaming with a mix of nostalgia and pride, "Pretty much, but with the help of some fine women." He added, his voice carrying the weight of history.

Bobby, standing near the door, gestured to Chuck sitting at the head of the table. "Alan, this is Chuck Langdon, our family attorney and close friend. Chuck, I'll let you lead this and review what we've discussed."

Chuck exchanged handshakes and said, "Alan, I understand the family has informed you of their intention to receive residuals from any use of their likeness in a television series."

Alan nodded, and Chuck continued. "While we understand this may not be a typical practice, it is non-negotiable. The document before you is straightforward and plain-spoken. The family will agree to a maximum of five episodes with no payment to any member of the Campbell Family; however, employees of family businesses portrayed will be paid custom industry rates. For each episode aired, the network will donate to the Campbell Family Foundation $50,000. Should the network wish to continue the series following the first five episodes, The Campbell Family will receive residuals in perpetuity, with future payments to the foundation increased to $75,000.

The family has agreed to one season or year of filming and will sign a contract to that effect if the prior demands are met."

Alan cleared his throat, sat upright in his chair, and said, "As I mentioned to Bobby last night, 'Reality' TV personalities aren't typically paid residuals. Residuals are negotiated by unions such as the Screen Actor's Guild (SAG)."

Chuck nodded, unfazed, "I understand that. I've researched this, and from what I've uncovered, it appears that reality TV stars are taken advantage of. While some may be paid well, they don't share any royalties. That doesn't seem fair at all. Well, that's the deal, Alan. Take it or leave it."

Alan acknowledged the firm offer and said, "I give you my word that I will do everything in my power to get this done."

After the meeting at the brewery, Brooks dropped the Kaplans off at the lake lodge and said before leaving, "Andy, Jenna's husband, will pick you folks up around 6:30 and drive you to the Bottom for the concert."

Once inside, Alan made himself a bourbon, his hands steady as he poured the liquid into the glass. He glanced over at Jennifer, raising an eyebrow. "Want a drink?" he asked, his voice carrying a hint of weariness.

A simple "Yes" followed. He made gin and tonic and handed it to her.

She said, "Thank you. Two lime wedges, just how I like it."

Alan returned her smile, a slight grin tugging at the corner of his lips. "I'm doing my best to impress."

She looked at him and rolled her eyes almost playfully, which caused butterflies in Alan's stomach for the first time in weeks.

She said, "I shared some personal details of our lives last night with the ladies. Believe it or not, you're not the only philanderer around here. Dottie said Alex fucked up as well a few years ago, and our new BFF, Brooks, is quite the cad as well. Julie said, and I quote, "Brooks will fuck anything hot and 'holler' from a gnat's ass to a horse collar."

Alan's eyes widened at the revelation. Jennifer gave him a stern look and said, "That's no excuse. It just means they are just as sorry as you, but Dottie helped me to see some things I'd been missing, so I'm committed to staying with you and fighting for what we have. I forgive you, Alan, and I'll do my best to forget it, not bring it up again, but I swear, if you ever do this shit again, I'll fucking ruin your ass." Her words hit Alan like a cold wave, and for a brief moment, his throat tightened. He hadn't expected this. But then, her voice softened, and she added, "I would have never believed you would cheat me on me, but I know I have some soul searching to do as well. So, let's try our best to put this behind us." Alan walked up to his wife with tears in his eyes, and they embraced for the first time in weeks. The weight of the past few days seemed to lift just a little as they stood there, a fragile truce between them.

Jennifer then said, changing the subject, "I can tell you're concerned about their offer."

Alan looked up, wiping his eyes and said, "I sure am. Residuals are unheard of in this business, but I suppose there's a first for everything. It's not unfair- what they are proposing. Jesus, they're more concerned with their foundation than themselves individually."

Alan took a long sip from his glass and continued, "Last night, I talked to Rooster, and he told me about the foundation. They've given away millions over the years to their community. Rooster said, if you ask John about it, he will say, 'You can't outgive God.' This family is something else- I mean really special."

Jennifer said. "I know how long you have been looking for the next big hit, and I think you've found it. You'll make it happen. You always do. Move your things to my bedroom and come cuddle with me while I take a nap?"

Alan said, "I like that idea."

Henry rode home with Jake after the brewery tour and was thrilled when asked to help set up for the gig at Booger Bottom.

Andy stopped by as planned and drove the short five-mile trip to the Bottom. When the Kaplans arrived, they found Jake, Joe, and their son finishing the setup on the outdoor stage. Henry saw his parents and waved. Alan and Jennifer went inside to grab a beer and found Bobby and Brooks at the bar, surrounded by friends. Bobby saw them and said, "Hey folks, y'all thirsty? Schneider is half off tonight."

The couple walked up, and Bobby introduced them as out-of-town guests, not wanting to disclose anything about the project Alan seemed so eager to pursue.

Jennifer asked, "Where is the rest of the band?"

Brooks said, "The boys better be setting up outside, and the girls are still home getting prettyfull."

She replied, "That shouldn't take long, those are some beautiful ladies." As if on cue, Dottie, Jenna, and Julie entered the bar to a round of applause.

Bobby said, "Hey, y'all didn't clap when Brooks and I walked in!" A male voice from the back yelled, "Y'all ain't as pretty as they are!"

Dottie wore a long-sleeved, dark sage-colored V-neck midi dress that shimmered subtly under the dim lights, complimented by an ivory scarf with sage and pink floral accents and brown boots. Her locks of curly, sandy hair were pulled back in a messy bun with pulled-out strands of curls flowing on each side. Jenna chose a V-neck long-sleeve chiffon in teal with brown accents, a wide brown belt, and brown boots with her wavy auburn hair fixed with a low ponytail and textured crown.

Jenna said, "Well, I'm sure glad to see my uncles dressed up for the occasion!" Bobby and Brooks both wore jeans, cowboy boots, and untucked long-sleeve ruffled tuxedo shirts. Bobby's was white satin, and Brooks' pale blue.

Dottie smiled, "I made them promise to dress the part. You'd be surprised how much I paid for those two shirts."

Brooks kissed her on the cheek and said, "We are grateful. Bobby is wearing his to work Monday."

Bobby said, "Alright, kids, y'all ready to get this show started?"

Brooks said, "Hell yeah!" He took one last swig from his beer, bent his neck back, his throat working as he gargled the last swallow, and said, "Just getting the pipes lubricated."

The Campbells walked on stage and found their respective places. Brooks took center stage with Jenna by his side. Dottie began the piano intro to Meatloaf's "Two Out of Three Ain't Bad." The spotlight hit Brooks just as he opened his mouth, and the crowd seemed to collectively hold their breath. Brooks began the vocals with Jenna singing backup. Alan and Jennifer found a spot up front and stood near center stage. As he listened to Brooks' rendition of the ballad, he was pleased with his decision to hire a local team to capture the event on video. He turned his head, looked wide-eyed at Jennifer, and slowly shook his head in disbelief at the talent.

The song ended, and the band transitioned to Stevie Nicks' and Don Henley's "Leather and Lace," where Dottie and Brooks covered vocals. The next up was Dottie singing another Fleetwood Mac classic, "Landslide," with Bobby picking the tune expertly on his Martin. Next were two Emmylou Harris numbers, "Boulder to Birmingham" and "C'est la Vie (You Never Can Tell)." The crowd was entranced, swaying together as one, as if united in the shared experience of the music.

When Dottie finished, Brooks walked to center stage and grabbed a mic. "My family and I would like to thank you for coming out tonight. I see a lot of familiar faces, but in case we've not met, I'd like to introduce our band. I'm Brooks Campbell. The handsome fella here on guitar is my brother, Bobby. On piano and vocals, my lovely sister and her beautiful and fiery daughter, Jenna. In the back on drums is Bobby's son, Joe, and on bass is my son, Jake. Schneider is half off tonight, so y'all drink up! Okay, ladies, if your man doesn't get off his feet and dance with you on these next two, he's not worth taking home!"

Bobby began the licks to Dobie Gray's "Drift Away' with Jake hammering the bass. Before Brooks began, he found Amy in the crowd and blew her a kiss. Brooks sang the first verse. On the chorus, the rest of the family joined in and harmonized beautifully.

Next up was Bobby covering guitar and vocals on Eric Clapton's "Wonderful Tonight." As Bobby sang, Jennifer and Alan slowly danced to the tune, holding each other closely. She whispered in his ear, "I can't wait any longer. I'm gonna need that dick when we get back to the lodge. The Campbell Brothers have got me wet!"

Alan laughed and whispered back, "Fuck! Me too! I need a damn Depends!"

A few songs later, the band performed The Band's "The Weight." Joe sang Levon Helm's intro with the rest of the family taking an additional verse The crowd was completely immersed, their energy feeding the rhythm of the song.

As the Campbells performed, Alan marveled at how picturesque the scene was. The stage is constructed under a stately oak tree draped in Spanish moss just feet from Lake Early's shoreline. The water glistened under the moonlight, casting ripples that danced to the beat of the music. A hearty round of applause echoed across the water as the song ended. Brooks, again at center stage, said, "We're gonna let the kids finish us off tonight." Bobby grabbed the Les Gibson, and Brooks took the Martin. The brothers began the intro, and Joe, still at his drums, closed his eyes and began the Eagles' classic, "Lying Eyes".

When he opened his eyes, he found Blake in the crowd and smiled. A moment of connection flashed between them – intimate, electric. She blew him a kiss, and his heart skipped a beat. The background vocals and harmonies were flawless. Jennifer looked at Alan and said, "I don't know when I've had such a fun weekend!" He agreed with a nod. Jake took the lead on "Take it to the Limit" and did a fine job of covering Randy Meisner's challenging vocals. As he sang, Amy locked eyes with him and mouthed, "I Love You." The next two were Joe covering The Eagles' "Take It Easy" and Jake with "Everything I Own" by the group Bread. The crowd swayed, drawn into the timeless charm of the music, their spirits lifted by the raw emotion in the voices.

The last song of the night was Jenna covering Linda Ronstadt's "Long Long Time" with her grandfather, John Campbell, playing the violin. Her voice was haunting, filled with a depth that seemed to echo through the ages, and when the final note lingered in the air, it was like time itself had paused.

As the band finished, Alan's mind was racing. His thoughts scattered like leaves in the wind. He barely slept the night before contemplating the family's precondition and knew he had an uphill battle with the network. Still, he was glad he hired a local videographer, with the family's permission, to capture the concert to take back. The elder Campbells came down from the stage and mingled with the crowd while Jake, Joe, and Andy packed up the gear. Alan noticed how the process flowed without direction.

As soon as the last set was over, the younger Campbells got right to work disassembling the stage and had it completed in less than 20 minutes. Henry informed Alan later that evening that he offered to help with packing, and Jake said thanks, but they had it covered." Alan replied, "I'm sure they were tired and ready to get home."

Henry replied, "Yeah, Jake told me on the way over that's the rules, the kids set up and clean up."

The Campbells said their goodbyes to the Kaplans as they left for Atlanta the following day to catch a flight to Phoenix. It was a bittersweet moment, full of unspoken sentiments, but they knew the bonds they forged that weekend would not be easily broken. On the trip back, Alan looked at the notes he made during the weekend. He organized the pictures, videos, and notes into a PowerPoint presentation. There was a quiet satisfaction in the process, the feeling of having captured something extraordinary, something that could change everything. He knew the network's leadership trusted his judgment, and with some good luck, he would have a crew filming soon.

Alan's first call on Monday morning was to Leo Weiland, Chief Executive Producer. Alan knew Leo was looking for the next big show, so he dangled the carrot. Alan said, "Leo, I've just returned from a weekend in South Georgia with my wife and son, and I have found what we've been looking for." As they talked, Alan shared his screen with Leo and introduced him to the family. He showed photos of the brewery, farm, and vet hospital and ended with a few seconds of video of the concert. As the video played, Alan watched Leo's face closely, looking for that spark, that moment when he would know he had hit the mark.

After watching the video, Alan said, "So, what do you think, Leo?" Leo was silent for a few seconds but responded, "Alan, this is it, boy! This is exactly what we've been looking for. Pure Americana, and what a helluva story they have!"

Alan said, "I couldn't agree more. The only issue is their demands." Alan detailed the conditions put forth by the family.

Leo replied, "So let me get this straight- they agree to five episodes with no payment but to their foundation- a tax write-off, and their employees?"

Alan answered, "Yes, but after that, residuals."

Leo replied, "May not be a problem. The SAG strike last year included support for reality TV performers. I'm unaware of any resolution that has been agreed upon yet, but this is a regular topic at board meetings. Everyone knows it's coming, so maybe we will be the first."

By 9:00 Wednesday morning, Leo phoned back and said, "We've Got A Show! The final details will be ironed out later, but you can let them know we have agreed to their terms of producing five shows with donations to their foundation. After that, we will negotiate further programming to include residual payments. How soon can you get started?"

Alan beamed with excitement and replied, "Within two weeks."

Leo replied, "Legal will have a contract ready by the end of the week."

Alan hung up the phone. He leaned back in his chair and closed his eyes for a few minutes of reflection, allowing the moment to sink in. Kaplan felt as if an enormous weight had been removed from his chest. A few minutes later, he texted Jennifer at work, sharing the good news. Jennifer, a dermatologist, is part owner of a practice in Phoenix. She called him back between patients, and Alan shared his excitement.

Jennifer said, grinning ear to ear, "Babe, I'm so happy for you and the Campbells. I just hope they are ready for the exposure."

Alan replied, "Yeah, right! I'm not sure if they know how famous they are about to become. I'm glad they have the gated entrance to their property because, well- you know."

While visiting the previous weekend, Alan was pleased to find the entrance to Campbell's property, where the homes are located is only accessible from one gated entrance. Alan's next call was to Bobby.

Bobby answered in his office as he was having lunch. "Hey Alan, I hope y'all had a pleasant enough trip back out west."

Alan responded, "Yes, and thanks. Bobby, I didn't think I would have news this soon, but I've been given the green light to produce five episodes with the proposal you shared." Bobby replied, "Wow, I wasn't expecting to hear back so soon. Hold on while I see if Brooks and Dottie can join in."

Bobby called each and added them to the call. Alan greeted both and relayed his discussions with Leo and the plan to complete a contract by week's end.

He asked, "OK folks, any last-minute jitters or reservations before we move forward? I know this is a lot to take in, so I want to ensure we are on the same page. Any questions?"

Brooks replied, "The contract is for the first five and nothing else, correct? If we don't feel comfortable after that, we can forego any future filming?"

Alan replied, "Exactly, but I sincerely hope you will choose to proceed.

The three Campbells agreed to move forward, and Alan described the next steps. "We would like to get started over the next two weeks with the pre-production." Alan detailed some pre-production items, including videoing and photographing the family and setting. A few more details were discussed, and the call ended. Bobby sent his siblings a group text, "Pump House After Work."

Later that day, Bobby, Julie, Dottie, Alex, and Brooks met at the Pump House. The four gathered on the back porch, leaning back in their chairs and cracking open an after-work beer. Bobby said, "This is a big step for our family. I want to make sure we are all on board." He looked around the group, his eyes searching for any signs of hesitation.

Julie responded, "It's a lot to consider. We all need to understand how this could affect our private lives." She raised an eyebrow, her fingers tapping nervously on her bottle.

Dottie chimed in, "Let's see how it goes. We are only committed to five episodes. That should give us enough experience to see if we want to move forward." She leaned forward, her hands clasped in front of her, trying to ease the tension in the air.

Brooks, taking a long pull from his beer, shrugged nonchalantly. "I don't see what we have to lose other than some privacy, and I'm not very private, but this is uncharted territory for all of us. I agree with Dottie. The first few episodes should give us an idea of what to expect. Fortunately, our houses are protected by the gate, so we shouldn't have to deal with weirdos just showing up. This is a great opportunity for the family foundation, so I'm excited to get it going."

Bobby nodded and said, "That's the primary reason for doing this."

# Chapter 25

The following week, a media crew arrived and began the pre-production tasks of capturing video and photos. Cameras were installed at the brewery, vet hospital, and Pump House.

The crew took pictures of each family member and shots of the Brewery, farm, vet hospital, and Pump House. Brooks tugged at his shirt collar, shifting awkwardly under the camera's gaze, his grin crooked but endearing. Rooster, in contrast, leaned casually against the barn door, arms folded across his chest, his expression a mix of mischief and pride. He gave a slow nod to the camera, tipping his hat with a wink as if he were the one in charge of the whole show.

Once the footage was complete, it was sent to Alan, who oversaw the editing. He worked late into the night; the soft glow of the monitor casting shadows on his focused face. Headphones pressed firmly over his ears, he moved through the footage with careful attention, making sure each scene flowed just right, as if the story was unfolding in his hands. The final product was an introductory video to the Campbell Family and their surroundings. It began with a few seconds of video of Lake Early at Sunset. A lone heron perched on a cypress stump, stretching its wings before gliding gracefully into the sky. The colors of the sunset deepened as the heron flew, its wings cutting through the sky like a quiet whisper. The title of the series appeared, "Chasing Sunsets." A faint soundtrack of frogs croaking, crickets chirping, and birds singing played, and the video transitioned to old photos of the early days of the farm and brewery as a recording of Bobby and Brooks picking and strumming a light melody played.

A recording of Rooster narrated as the antique black and white photos of the Schneiders and Youngs were displayed on the screen- "In the 1890s, German and Scottish immigrants, the Schneiders and Young, settled in Sullivan County, Georgia along the Thronateeska River. They soon built a thriving farm and brewery which remains in operation today." The voice of Rooster was warm and steady, carrying a weight of history that seemed to hang in the air.

"In 1910, another Scott arrived, Asa Campbell, who married into the Young Family- Photos of Asa, Katie, and their children were portrayed and changed to photos of the Campbells of today. Today, the Campbell Family operates one of the largest privately owned breweries in the USA along with a thriving farm and veterinary practice." The screen transitioned to the Campbells on the front porch of John's home. The music faded, and the Campbells introduced themselves. After the last one, Jake spoke, they all, in unison, loudly said, "We're the Campbells of Sullivan County; thanks for stopping by!" The editing was completed in a week and shown to the Campbells for their approval. They gathered around the screen, watching intently, and when it ended, they exchanged smiles of satisfaction, knowing the beginning had been just right.

Filming for the series began within two weeks. The first few days were somewhat awkward, with everyone trying to get used to the cameras. But before long, the nerves wore off, and by the second week, things were pretty much back to normal. Alan told the family to pretend like the cameras weren't there. "Just be yourselves", he said.

A crew of one filmed the day-to-day operation of the vet practice and captured Clover as she examined an elderly Labrador Retriever. The old Lab had skin allergies, and Clover gave her a low-dose steroid.

"I've been treating this girl for years for her allergies," Clover said, gently rubbing the dog's head. She turned to the owner and asked, "How old is Lilly now?"

The owner responded, "She just had her 10th birthday."

Clover patted Lilly on her head and said, "Many vets don't believe in low-dose steroids for skin allergies, but I do. For some animals, there's simply nothing else that works. There are more expensive injections, but in my experience, they are hit-and-miss. Without the meds, Lilly would be living in pure agony. For me and most owners, we choose quality of life over quantity."

The camera then shifted to Dottie, who was treating a mixed-breed pit bull who was brought in with a large laceration on his left side. The dog had a large wild boar cornered, and the pig ripped the skin as it went in for the kill. Dottie quickly anesthetized the dog and cleaned the wound before sewing. "God, what I would give if wild hogs and coyotes had never made their way to Georgia." She muttered under her breath, shaking her head as she worked.

Next, the crew filmed Brooks and Jamey at the cattle working facilities, where 25 weaned calves were caught up for vaccines and castrations. The camera operator filmed as Brooks sliced the scrotum of a four-month-old bull and removed his gonads in less than 30 seconds. The testicles were placed in a small cooler, and Brooks turned to the camera with a grin, "If you've never had calf fries, you're missing out."

Suddenly, a loud bang was heard, and everyone looked up to see the source of the noise. Apparently, a bull calf wanted nothing to do with the day's events and decided to charge the ten-foot gate— the only thing keeping the animals confined. With a surprising burst of strength, the young bull tore the gate from the hinges and ran a hundred yards across the pasture with the gate still around its neck.

Jamey broke the silence, "Well, would you just look at that muthafucka. Run damn you run you son-of-a-bitch! I hope you break your fuckin neck! Brookie, I told you last week that bastard was gonna be a problem."

Brooks stood there for a moment, shaking his head in disbelief. He pointed a bloody hand, still holding the knife, and said, "That shit- that shit right there is why we eat them and their fuckin balls!"

The crew couldn't help but laugh, the moment feeling a little less like work and a lot more like life on the farm.

In the second month of filming, Bobby and Libby were in the brewery conference room on a Zoom call with their ad agency. Libby's hand absentmindedly tapped the edge of her coffee mug, and Bobby leaned back in his chair, crossing his arms, his brow furrowed in thought. The call was centered around getting the brand more exposure outside the Southeast. Different ideas were tossed around when a young rep from the agency asked if they would consider promoting or endorsing Gay Pride Month with their brand.

Libby paused, her eyes narrowing slightly. She exchanged a look with Bobby, a half-crooked smile tugging at the corner of her lips as though she already knew the answer, thinking to herself, 'This should be good.'. Bobby let out a long sigh, rolled his eyes and said, "That's not happening. The Schneider brand doesn't promote anything outside of our beer. We don't take sides- one way or the other on social issues, no matter how thrilling the subject may be."

The young ad rep continued to press. "Mr. Campbell, you could be missing a real opportunity here. Most beer brands you compete with have embraced the LGBTQ community."

Bobby's face hardened, his jaw tightening as he leaned forward slightly. "I'll tell you what, young lady, here's my response to that, 'We don't care who you fuck, we just care what you drink!' Put that on the fuckin' carton!" He slammed his hand down on the desk, the sudden force of it echoing in the room. Libby Maddox had worked for Bobby for years and certainly knew of his short fuse and wasn't alarmed in the least by his response. Knowing the cameras were rolling, she simply put her hand over her forehead to cover her struggle to keep from breaking out in laughter from Bobby's comment.

Dove season in Georgia opens annually on the first Saturday in September, and a yearly tradition is an opening day hunt on the Campbell property. A 30-acre field is planted in strips of sunflowers, wheat, millet, and grain sorghum. The scent of the earth still fresh from the late summer heat, the field stands tall and proud, waiting for its moment in the spotlight. In mid-August, the field is strip-mowed and burned the week before the shoot.

John started the tradition in the mid-70s as a corporate outing for the brewery's employees. A few close friends, such as the Langdon's, are invited, but mostly the Campbells, their employees and a couple of vendors. Two cameras rolled during the shoot but stayed hidden behind ground blinds for camouflage, capturing the quiet intensity of the hunt. The air was thick with anticipation; the only sounds were the occasional rustle of leaves and the distant call of birds overhead. Bobby assigned hunter positions based on numbers drawn from a hat. The tension of the moment was clear on everyone's faces as they waited for the first sign of movement.

Early September is still summer in South Georgia, but this year was pleasant, with highs in the low-80s, low humidity, and calm breezes.

Bobby stood in front of the group, clearing his throat as he prepared to speak, "My family and I would like to thank you for coming, and we hope you have a great time. We've been blessed with some fine weather for opening day, so let's have some fun, but safety first." His eyes scanned the group, landing on the younger hunters. "I see a lot of young hunters here today. Dads, keep yours' and the kid's barrels high. No shooting at low birds! If you do so, you're off the field. Everyone should know the bird limits; if you go over, that's between you and the game warden."

After sunset, the group headed to the brewery pavilion to feast on barbeque, the air filled with the savory aroma of smoked pork. John, who had been tending to the fire all day, wiped his hands on his apron and looked over at Rooster, both grinning with satisfaction at their work. John raises a couple of pigs each year for the barbeque. He and Rooster had been cooking since dawn, and it was ready to eat by sundown. The Campbell ladies brought sides and joined the men for UGA football on TV. Everyone settled in; most with beer in hand, and the familiar hum of conversation filled the space. The season's first game was UGA vs The Tennessee School for the Blind. No, but you get the idea- not a serious competitor. It was the first game, so everyone watched the kickoff and the first few plays. However, with the score being so lopsided, the crowd lost interest and scattered along the property, drinking beer and visiting with old friends and new.

A camera zeroed in on Jamey Jones, who was leaning back against a fence, his arms crossed, and a mischievous grin plastered across his face as he told a story about his recent run-in with the law. His hand instinctively clutched his chest like he was about to give a solemn confession: "May God strike me blind boys if I'm lying." Jamey said with a dramatic pause, his eyes wide as if to make the moment even more ridiculous. "I had no idea you needed muthafuckin stickers for a muthafuckin canoe with a muthafuckin trolling motor."

Brooks, who was leaning against a nearby tree, snorted in amusement, rolling his eyes before adding his two cents, "Hell, don't forget about indecent exposure."

Jamey's expression instantly changed to mock offense, his hand coming up to his forehead like he had just remembered something truly scandalous. "Damn right! I forgot about that shit. The muthafucka comes up to my right around a clump of trees while I'm taking a piss off the side." He said, shaking his head with exasperation. "He said he could charge me with indecent exposure. I asked that muthafucka, who said it wasn't decent?"

The crowd laughed, and Brooks chuckled, his voice dripping with sarcasm as he leaned in with a smirk, "You probably just pissed him off when he saw that damn dick." Jamey is known around the farm for being exceptionally blessed between the legs.

Jamey replied, "Probably so. You know them law dogs have a reputation for being of the small dick variety." He looked and pointed at Grady and said, "That's why they fuck with the black man so much."

Grady, who had been quietly sipping his beer, snorted in disbelief and looked over with a smirk and wide eyed, "The hell you say!"

Jamey grinned and leaned in as though imparting deep wisdom, "Damn right. They see a black man and think to themselves, 'That muthafucka got a dick bigger than mine. I just know it."

The group laughed, and one of the surgeons from Grady's practice, Michael Ruben, said, "You know, Jamey, you really may be on to something. I mean, when have you seen a Jewish guy being arrested on 'Cops'? Fucking never!"

One episode of the series was centered on the holidays. The camera smoothly zoomed in as the family gathered at their Bahamian estate for Thanksgiving, the golden sunset casting a warm glow over the beach as they dived into lobstering, feasted on fresh seafood, and laughed together, the sound of music playing softly at the Conch.

Then, the scene shifted to the brewery for the employee Christmas Party and John and Clover's for the family's Christmas. The Christmas episode showed the family centered around the piano in the home's living room. They sang ancient carols and a few modern songs. One of John Campbell's favorites is The Band's, "Christmas Must Be Tonight." A proud smile crossed his face as he shared this with the film crew, his fondness for the song clear. The Band is a favorite of John Campbell's. A light chuckle escaped his lips as he remembered that one special moment with Madie. A sense of pride for John is that he and Madie saw The Band's last concert. During filming, John told of how he and Madie travelled to San Francisco during Thanksgiving in 1976 to see the group's farewell performance at the Winterland Ballroom.

He said, "Rarely in history has so much musical talent been together on a single stage." He went on describing how the entire concert was filmed by Martin Scorsese and released in 1978 with a cult following to this day.

The first five episodes were completed in less than eight months. Alan flew back to Georgia to meet with the family for some final editing before the series was broadcast on the network.

Alan said, "Guys, I can't tell you how much I've enjoyed working on this project and being invited into your lives. Jennifer, Henry and I have come to consider your family close friends, and we thank God our paths crossed." He placed a hand over his heart, his voice thick with gratitude. "I wanted to tell you all that face to face. That's one reason I wanted to come here, but I also wanted to tell you in person the results of our initial press screenings. The feedback couldn't be more positive. Everyone agrees this is the show America is looking for. There's so much division in the nation today, and your sweet family can only add some calm." The three Campbells thanked Alan for his kind remarks and returned the sentiment.

Dottie asked, "So when will the series air?"

Alan replied, "We plan to air the first episode in late July to early August."

The series premiered on July 30. The night of the premiere, the air was thick with excitement as the family and close friends gathered at John and Clover's. The night was festive and included an all-family swim in the pool following the showing. The date fell on a Thursday, and everyone took the next day off.

The next day, America woke up to what could only be described as "Campbell Mania." Media companies from North Florida to Atlanta showed up at the brewery and vet hospital, hoping to catch a glimpse of the family. The network predicted the onslaught of attention and had representatives onsite to assist the family in dealing with the reporters. The family took it in stride, and each one made themselves available. Bobby and Brooks kept post at the brewery, and Dottie, Clover, and John at the vet hospital and store.

By Christmas, the family and the network had agreed to more episodes, and a new contract was drawn up. The family's attention was more than expected, and some adjustments had to be made for security, but nothing interfered with the family's day-to-day lives. John, Clover, Joe and Jake received hundreds of marriage proposals, but each was politely declined. The family made a few public appearances but mostly stayed to their roots in Southwest Georgia. Brooks had a few t-shirts made for the family with the Schneider Brand and the quote from Bobby, "We Don't Care Who You F#@%, We Just Care What You Drink." At the next show at Booger Bottom, the guys wore them onstage.

The Campbell family's foundation grew exponentially after the series aired. A new wing was built on the Sullivan County Hospital in memory of Madie. Tears welled up in the eyes of many as the dedication ceremony took place. Several more scholarships were added, and the local animal shelters were given $50,000 each for new kennels and updated facilities.

Joe and Blake married last summer after building a modest home near Brooks' place. Jake finished college and joined Brooks on the farm and brewery full-time. Jenna finished vet school and joined her mom at the vet hospital. Clover has primarily retired but still works a few days per month. Last Sunday, the entire family went out on the pontoon for an early spring sunset cruise. The boat gently rocked on the calm waters as the family gathered around, laughter floating on the breeze. They stopped a mile north of the lake lodge and settled in as one of Lake Early's finest sunsets appeared on the west horizon. The orange and pink hues painted the sky, and the family grew quiet, each lost in their own thoughts. As the sun lowered and the colors exploded, John said to his family, "Kids, this is what it's all about: loving each other and chasing sunsets."

The End

# About The Author

Ask anyone who knows him and they'll say, "John Ruffin is a **storyteller**". Whether tending to the cattle on his **family's centennial farm in Central Georgia** or retreating to his **sanctuary on Lake Blackshear**, Ruffin finds inspiration in the **stillness of the water, the crackle of a hilltop fire, or the majesty of a sunset.**

A deeply **spiritual man**, he embraces **meditation, nature, and the art of reflection**—drawing strength from the land and the timeless rhythms of the world around him. His love for his **family, farm, dogs, and moments of quiet connection with the environment** fuel both his personal journey and his storytelling.

With **Chasing Sunsets**, Ruffin brings readers a novel steeped in **emotion, resilience, and the beauty of second chances**. His stories are not just written—they are **lived, felt, and deeply rooted in the soul.**

*"Close families aren't by accident, they're by design."*

– John Ruffin